SWEET PAPER FLOWERS

A SWEET COVE MYSTERY
BOOK 25

J. A. WHITING

To hear about new books and book sales, please sign up for my mailing list at:
jawhiting.com

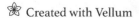 Created with Vellum

With thanks to my readers

Use your magic for good

1

The autumn sun streamed through the large windows of the Victorian mansion's high-end kitchen, spreading light over the gleaming stainless steel appliances and the polished granite counter-tops. The four Roseland sisters - Angie, Jenna, Ellie, and Courtney - along with their husbands and their adopted family member Mr. Finch, were gathered around the spacious island, sipping coffee from mismatched mugs and nibbling on a marble cake Angie had made earlier in the day.

Perched atop the refrigerator, Euclid and Circe, the family's feline companions, watched the scene below them with keen interest. Euclid's orange fur seemed to glow in the sunlight, while Circe's black coat shimmered, the small white spot on her chest standing out like a tiny star.

"Oh, look at this one," Jenna exclaimed, pointing at a photo of Courtney and Rufus cutting their wedding cake. "Angie, you can see how beautiful your cake was in this shot."

Angie bent closer to look, her honey blonde hair fell in soft waves around her shoulders. "It did turn out well, didn't it?" she said with a little bit of pride. "But nothing could outshine our beautiful bride and handsome groom."

Courtney's cheeks tinged pink, her hair pulled back in a loose bun. "Stop it. You'll make me blush more than I did at the wedding."

"I don't think that's possible," Rufus chimed in, his English accent adding charm to his words. He wrapped an arm around his wife's waist and planted a kiss on her cheek.

"Now, now, let's not embarrass the newlyweds too much," Mr. Finch said with a twinkle in his eye. "Though I must say, it's a joy to see you both so happy."

Ellie flipped to another photo, this one showing all four sisters together. "I love this one," she said softly. "We all look so happy."

"We were," Angie agreed. "Are," she corrected herself with a smile.

Josh, Angie's husband, gestured to another photo. "This one's great, too," he said, showing a candid shot of Mr. Finch dancing with his girlfriend, Betty Hayes.

Mr. Finch adjusted the collar of his white shirt, looking slightly flustered. "Well, I may be old, but I can still cut a rug when the occasion calls for it."

Everyone laughed, the sound of their mirth filling the kitchen with warmth.

"I still can't believe the wedding went so perfectly," Angie said, her blue eyes sparkling with joy for her youngest sister.

Courtney beamed with happiness. "It really was magical," she agreed, twisting her new wedding band around her finger. "Rufus and I couldn't have asked for a more beautiful day."

Jenna said, "The weather was perfect, the flowers were gorgeous, and don't even get me started on that cake, Angie. You outdid yourself."

Tom, Jenna's husband, added, "And let's not forget the venue. That yacht was absolutely beautiful."

"It really was," Ellie chimed in. "Jack and I were

just saying how romantic it all looked under those twinkling lights."

Jack, Ellie's always formally dressed husband, nodded in agreement. "I have to admit, I was a bit worried about getting seasick, but thankfully, I didn't, and I was able to enjoy the evening," he said with a wry smile.

"Oh, you," Ellie said, playfully swatting his arm.

Angie looked at her youngest sister. "You looked absolutely stunning in your wedding dress. Mom would have been so proud."

A moment of bittersweet silence fell over the kitchen as the sisters remembered their mother. Euclid let out a soft meow, as if sensing the change in emotions.

"She was there with us, I'm sure of it," Courtney said softly, her eyes misting slightly.

Rufus squeezed her hand. "Of course she was, love. And I'm sure she's thrilled to bits about having me as a son-in-law," he added with a cheeky grin.

The group chuckled again, the somber moment broken.

"So, Courtney," Ellie said, her blue eyes twinkling mischievously, "how does it feel to be Mrs. Fudge?"

Courtney giggled, a sound of pure joy. "Honestly? It feels wonderful. Rufus is..." she paused, searching for the right word. "He's just perfect. I never thought I could be this happy."

"We're so thrilled for you both," Jenna said, reaching out to squeeze her sister's hand. "You and Rufus were made for each other."

"Indeed," Mr. Finch said sagely. "It's a rare and beautiful thing to find your perfect match."

"That's a wonderful sentiment," Rufus said, looking touched.

As the morning wore on, the group continued to reminisce about the wedding, sharing favorite moments and laughing over small mishaps that now seemed funny in hindsight.

"Remember when Betty almost fell into the punch bowl?" Angie said, wiping tears of laughter from her eyes.

"Oh gosh, yes," Courtney replied, barely able to speak through her giggles. "If it hadn't been for Tom's quick reflexes..."

"We'd have had a very pink-tinted guest at the reception," Rufus finished, chuckling.

As the laughter died down, Josh glanced at his watch. "I hate to break this up, but I've got a meeting at the resort in twenty minutes."

"I should get to the bake shop," Angie added, standing up. "Those muffins won't bake themselves."

One by one, they began to disperse to tend to their various businesses and responsibilities. Courtney and Rufus were the last to leave, lingering in the kitchen doorway.

"It's been wonderful, hasn't it?" Courtney said softly, looking back at the now-empty kitchen.

"It sure has," Rufus agreed. "I love being part of this family."

Courtney leaned into him, feeling a wave of contentment wash over her. "And I love you being part of it."

With one last look at the sun-filled kitchen, where Euclid and Circe were now curled up together in a patch of sunlight, Courtney and Rufus headed out to start their days.

Angie made her way to her bakery, the Sweet Dreams Bake Shop, which occupied part of the Victorian mansion. The scent of vanilla and cinnamon greeted her as she entered, and she inhaled deeply, feeling lucky to have her shop.

She had just finished arranging a tray of freshly baked blueberry muffins in the display case when the bell above the door chimed. Angie looked up to see a woman she didn't recognize enter the bake shop.

The newcomer was tall and slender with short, spiky brown hair and keen hazel eyes that seemed to take in every detail of the bakery. She wore a crisp light blue shirt tucked into dark jeans with a leather messenger bag slung across her shoulder.

As soon as the woman stepped inside, Angie felt a strange sensation wash over her. It was as if a cold breeze had suddenly blown through the warm shop. She shivered involuntarily, feeling a sense of anxiety and unease that she couldn't explain.

Pushing the feeling aside, Angie put on her best welcoming smile. "Good morning. Welcome to the Sweet Dreams Bake Shop. What can I get for you today?"

The woman approached the counter, her eyes still roaming around the shop. "Hello," she said, her voice low and slightly husky. "I've heard wonderful things about your pastries. I'd love a coffee and ... what would you recommend?"

"Well, our blueberry muffins just came out of the oven," Angie suggested, gesturing to the tray she had just set out. "They're still warm."

"Perfect," the woman said. "I'll take one of those and a large black coffee, please."

As Angie prepared the order, the feeling of unease returned. Her intuition, usually so reliable, was sending mixed signals. There was something about this woman that felt off, somehow, but at the same time, Angie sensed no immediate danger or ill intent.

"Here you are," Angie said, setting the coffee and muffin on the counter before ringing up the sale.

The woman handed over a bill. "Keep the change," she said with a smile, as she sat down on one of the stools near the counter. "I'm Lorrie, by the way. Lorrie Henderson. I'm new to town."

"Welcome to Sweet Cove," Angie replied, her natural friendliness overcoming her unease. "I'm Angie Roseland. Have you moved to Sweet Cove or are you here on vacation?"

Lorrie shook her head as she picked up her coffee. "I'm only here for a while. I'm a writer, actually. I'm here researching for my next book."

Angie's curiosity was piqued. "Oh? What kind of book is it?"

"True crime," Lorrie explained, taking a sip of her coffee. "I'm working on a book about a cold case that happened here in Sweet Cove about forty years ago. The murder of Karen LeBlanc. Have you heard of it?"

Angie frowned slightly, trying to recall. "The name sounds vaguely familiar, but I don't know much about it. I wasn't even born when it happened."

Lorrie nodded. "Karen was twenty-nine years old, staying in Sweet Cove for the months of June and July. She was found dead in her rental cottage. The case was never solved."

A chill ran down Angie's spine at the matter-of-fact way Lorrie described the murder. "That's terrible," she murmured.

"It is," Lorrie agreed. "That's why I'm here to try and piece together what happened. I like to stay in the locations where the crimes I write about took place. It helps me get a feel for the setting, the atmosphere."

Angie wasn't quite sure how to respond. The uneasy feeling in her stomach had returned and intensified.

"This is delicious, by the way," Lorrie said, gesturing at her half-eaten muffin. "I can see why everyone raves about your baking."

"Thanks so much," Angie replied. "I'm glad you're enjoying it."

They chatted for a few more minutes about

Sweet Cove and its attractions before Lorrie finished her coffee and prepared to leave.

"It was nice meeting you, Angie," Lorrie said as she headed for the door. "I'm sure I'll be back for more of these muffins."

As the door opened and closed with Lorrie's departure, Angie took a deep breath. She busied herself with wiping down the counter, trying to shake off the strange feelings Lorrie's visit had stirred up.

A few minutes later, Angie looked up to see Courtney entering the bakery.

"Hey, sis, what's cookin'?" Courtney called out cheerfully. "I thought I'd stop in to get a cookie."

Angie smiled at her sister. "Actually, I'm glad you're here. Something odd just happened."

Courtney's eyebrows rose with interest as she removed a cookie from the glass case. "Oh? Tell me."

Angie recounted her interaction with Lorrie Henderson, describing the unsettling feelings she'd experienced and some details about the cold case.

Courtney listened as Angie spoke. When her sister finished, she was quiet for a moment, seemingly lost in thought.

"A forty-year-old unsolved murder in Sweet Cove," Courtney mused, "and now a true crime writer shows up to investigate it. Angie, do you think...?"

Angie met her sister's gaze, understanding the unspoken question. "I don't know, but I felt really anxious when she was here talking to me."

Courtney said, "I hate to say it, but there might be a new mystery about to pull us in."

As if in response to Courtney's words, there was a sudden clatter from the back kitchen. Both sisters turned to see Euclid sitting on the counter, his large orange paw resting on a spoon he had just knocked over. His eyes seemed to bore into them with an intensity that sent a shiver over Angie's skin.

"Get down, Euclid. You can't be on the kitchen counter." Courtney gestured to the floor.

"I think," Angie replied slowly to her sister's question, "that whether we like it or not, we might be about to get involved in something new."

Courtney reached out and gave her sister's arm a little squeeze. "Well, whatever it is, we'll get through it. I was sort of hoping we wouldn't have a new crime to work on so soon." She squared her shoulders and smiled hopefully. "Maybe it's nothing. Maybe there isn't a crime or a mystery for us to work on just yet."

As the morning sun began to slant through the

bakery windows, sending shadows across the floor, the sisters shared a look

"You know," Courtney said, breaking the momentary silence, "I was looking forward to a quiet few weeks after the wedding. Rufus and I were talking about maybe taking a short trip to the Cape."

Angie smiled sympathetically. "I know. You should go. Like you said, this might be nothing. Just an author doing research for her book."

"But you don't believe that, do you?" Courtney asked with narrowed eyes, knowing her sister too well.

Angie sighed. "I want to, but..."

Courtney's expression turned serious. "Well, then we'll just have to see what happens. Maybe we should tell the others about this at dinner tonight?"

"Good idea," Angie agreed. "Better to have everyone on alert, just in case."

As they continued to discuss the situation, customers came and went, filling the bakery with the buzz of conversation. Despite the busy day, Angie kept feeling that something significant was about to be set in motion.

As the day wound down and Angie prepared to close the shop, she was lost in thought. The cold case, the author, the unsettling feelings ... they all swirled in her mind like the ingredients of a complicated recipe. Just like with her baking, Angie knew all these elements would eventually come together to form something new. Whether that something would be sweet or bitter remained to be seen.

With a final glance around the now-quiet bakery, Angie turned off the lights and locked the door. As she walked back to the main part of the Victorian, she resolved to stay alert and trust her instincts. After all, in their lives, one never knew when the next mystery might be just around the corner.

2

It was late afternoon when the four Roseland sisters, Mr. Finch, and the family cats gathered on the spacious front porch to enjoy the breeze. The wooden floorboards creaked softly under the gentle sway of the rocking chairs, and their rhythmic motion was as soothing as the chirping of birds in the nearby trees.

Angie, her hair pulled back in a loose ponytail, took a sip of her iced tea, her hand wet from the condensation beading on the glass.

"This is really nice," she said, her eyes taking in the peaceful scene before them of the wide green lawn and people strolling down the sidewalk to the white sand beach. "It's been too long since we've all had a chance to just sit and relax like this."

Jenna nodded in agreement, a few strands of her long brown hair dancing in the light breeze. "It really has. Between the wedding planning and all our businesses, it's been a whirlwind lately."

Courtney, still basking in newlywed bliss, smiled contentedly. "I couldn't agree more. Though I have to say, I'm loving every minute of married life so far."

Mr. Finch chuckled, his eyes twinkling behind his glasses. "Ah, young love. It does my heart good to see you so happy, Miss Courtney."

Euclid, the large orange Maine Coon, stretched lazily on the porch railing while Circe, curled up at Ellie's feet. The peaceful atmosphere was suddenly interrupted when Ellie stood up abruptly, nearly spilling her tea.

"I'm going to put on some coffee for Chief Martin," she announced, heading for the door.

The others exchanged knowing glances. Courtney rolled her eyes good-naturedly. "There she goes again. She doesn't even know she's doing it."

Angie, Mr. Finch, and Jenna chuckled in unison. They all knew about Ellie's uncanny ability to sense when Chief Martin was about to arrive, even if Ellie herself wasn't always aware of it.

"Do you think we should tell her what she's doing?" Jenna asked, a mischievous glint in her eye.

"Nah," Angie replied with a grin. "It's more fun this way."

A few minutes later, the distant rumble of an engine caught their attention. A police cruiser turned into the long driveway, kicking up a small cloud of dust as it approached the house.

"Right on cue," Mr. Finch murmured with a smile.

As if summoned by the sound, Ellie reappeared on the porch carefully balancing a tray laden with a coffee pot, cream, sugar, and several mugs. She set it down on the small table just as Chief Phillip Martin climbed the porch steps.

The Chief was a sturdy man in his late fifties with salt-and-pepper hair and kind eyes that crinkled at the corners when he smiled. Despite his imposing stature, there was a gentleness about him that put people at ease. He was dressed in his usual uniform, the badge on his chest catching the fading sunlight.

Euclid and Circe both perked up at the chief's arrival, padding over to greet him with friendly meows. Chief Martin bent down to scratch behind their ears, a fond smile on his face.

"Afternoon, everyone," he said, straightening up. "I hope I'm not interrupting anything."

"Not at all, Chief," Angie replied warmly. "Come have a seat. Ellie's just made some fresh coffee."

The chief settled into one of the vacant rocking chairs with a grateful sigh. "You always seem to know just what I need," he said, accepting a steaming mug from Ellie.

The sisters silently acknowledged the truth in his words. They had a long history with Chief Martin, dating back to their grandmother's time. He was well aware of the sisters' unique paranormal abilities and had often sought their help on difficult cases.

"So, what brings you by today, Chief?" Courtney asked. "Not that we don't always enjoy your company, but I have a feeling this isn't just a social call."

Chief Martin's expression turned serious as he took a sip of his coffee. "You're right. I'm afraid I'm here on official business." He paused, his eyes sweeping over the group. "There's been a murder in Sweet Cove, and I could use your help."

A hush fell over the porch, broken only by the sudden hiss from both Euclid and Circe. The cats' fur stood on end, their tails puffed up in agitation.

"A murder?" Jenna echoed, her voice barely above a whisper.

Chief Martin said, "I'm afraid so. It happened

earlier today. The victim is a retired English professor named Frank Sleet. He and his wife, Kris Moran-Sleet, had recently moved to town."

Angie felt a chill run down her spine, remembering her uneasy encounter with Lorrie Henderson earlier that day. "What happened?" she asked, her voice tight with concern.

The chief's face was somber as he continued. "Mrs. Moran-Sleet came home from grocery shopping and found her husband dead in their kitchen. He'd been shot."

As a collective gasp rose from the group, Mr. Finch shook his head sadly. "Such a tragedy. It seems they barely had time to settle in and this happened. How awful."

"That's terrible," Ellie murmured, her eyes wide with shock. "Do you have any leads?"

Chief Martin sighed heavily. "That's where things get complicated. There was something odd about the crime scene." He paused, his brow furrowing. "There were several paper flowers placed near the body."

As soon as the words left the chief's mouth, Angie felt a cold shiver run over her arms. The uneasy sensation she'd had earlier grew stronger, and she had the feeling this was somehow connected to Lorrie Henderson's arrival in town.

"Paper flowers?" Courtney repeated, her voice filled with confusion. "What do you mean?"

"Exactly that," Chief Martin replied. "Delicate, intricately folded paper flowers. They weren't just scattered around; they seemed to have been placed deliberately. It's not like anything I've ever seen before."

Mr. Finch's expression was thoughtful. "It sounds like some sort of calling card or signature. Perhaps our killer fancies himself an artist of sorts?"

Jenna shuddered at the thought. "That's chilling. To think someone would treat murder as a form of art..."

"That's why I'm here," Chief Martin said, his tone serious. "I know you all have unique perspectives that could be invaluable in a case like this. Your intuitions, your ability to sense things others might miss – I could really use your help on this one."

The sisters had assisted the chief many times before, but each new case brought its own challenges and dangers.

Angie was the first to speak. "Of course, we'll help. We're always here to lend a hand."

The others nodded in agreement.

"Absolutely," Courtney added. "Whatever we can do, we're on it."

Chief Martin's shoulders relaxed slightly, relief evident on his face. "Thank you. I knew I could count on you all. I'd like you to come and take a look at the crime scene tomorrow morning, if possible. Sometimes you pick up on things that even our best investigators miss."

"We'll be there," Ellie assured him. "What time should we come by?"

As they discussed the details for the following day, Angie's mind wandered back to her encounter with Lorrie Henderson. The timing seemed too coincidental – a true crime writer arrived in town to research an old cold case, and suddenly there's a new murder with strange clues left behind.

"Chief," Angie said, interrupting the conversation, "there's something else you should know. A woman came into my bakery today – a writer named Lorrie Henderson. She said she was in town researching an old cold case for a true crime book."

Chief Martin's eyebrows shot up. "A cold case? Did she mention which one?"

Angie told him, "She said it was about the murder of a woman named Karen LeBlanc, about forty years ago. Does that ring any bells?"

The chief's face darkened. "Karen LeBlanc ... now that's a name I haven't heard in a long time. It was before my time on the force, but every cop in Sweet Cove knows about that case. It's the one that got away, so to speak."

"Do you think there could be a connection between the writer looking into the case and Professor Sleet's murder?" Jenna asked with a serious expression.

Chief Martin shook his head slowly. "It's too early to say, but in my experience, there's no such thing as a coincidence in murder cases. I'll definitely look into this Lorrie Henderson."

As the conversation continued, the sun dipped lower in the sky. The peaceful afternoon had transformed into something more ominous with the murder and its mysterious circumstances hanging in the air.

Euclid and Circe, usually calm and composed, remained on edge, their tails twitching nervously. The cats' behavior didn't go unnoticed by the sisters, who knew better than to ignore such signs.

"There's something else," Mr. Finch said suddenly, his voice quiet but firm.

All eyes turned to him.

"When you mentioned the paper flowers, I had a

... feeling. It's hard to describe, but it was as if I could see them for a moment. The flowers seemed to be hiding something."

The sisters shared knowing looks. Mr. Finch's visions, while sometimes cryptic, often held important clues.

"The flowers might be hiding something?" Chief Martin repeated, his interest piqued. "What do you mean, Victor?"

Mr. Finch shook his head, his frustration evident on his face. "I'm not sure. It was just a flash, really, but I got the sense that the flowers themselves might contain some kind of message or clue."

"We'll make sure to examine them closely tomorrow morning," Angie assured him, reaching out to pat the man's hand gently.

As the afternoon wore on, Chief Martin filled them in on more details of the case, careful not to reveal anything that might compromise the investigation. As the sisters listened, each one made mental notes to try to piece together the puzzle.

Finally, as the sky was painted with pinks and violet, Chief Martin stood to leave. "Thank you all again," he said, his gratitude evident in his voice. "I'm lucky to have you on the case."

"You know we love a good mystery," Courtney

assured him. "Sweet Cove is our home, and we'll do what we can to keep it safe."

As they watched the chief's cruiser disappear down the driveway, a serious mood settled over the porch. The peaceful afternoon they'd been enjoying seemed like a distant memory now.

"Well," Angie said, "I guess we'd better get some rest. Tomorrow's going to be a long day."

The others murmured in agreement, gathering empty glasses and coffee cups. As they headed inside, Angie paused at the doorway, looking back at the now-quiet street. A gentle breeze rustled the leaves of the old oak tree in the front yard, and for a moment, she could have sworn she saw a flicker of movement in the shadows.

Shaking off the uneasy feeling, Angie stepped inside, closing the door firmly behind her. As she climbed the stairs to her suite of rooms, she had the feeling this case was going to be unlike anything they'd encountered before.

3

There was a slight chill in the early morning air when the Roseland sisters and Mr. Finch arrived at the Sleet residence in Ellie's van. The suburban home, with its neatly trimmed lawn and cheerful flower beds, seemed an unlikely setting for such a grim event. Yellow police tape fluttered in the breeze, cordoning off the house and yard while the investigation was ongoing.

Chief Martin stood waiting for them at the edge of the property, his usual friendly demeanor replaced by a serious expression. "Good morning, everyone," he greeted them, his voice low. "Thank you for coming so early."

Angie noticed movement behind the curtains in

one of the neighboring houses. "Looks like we have an audience," she murmured to Jenna, who nodded in response.

"Small-town curiosity, for sure." Chief Martin sighed. "Can't be helped. Now, before we go in, I need to remind you not to touch anything without gloves. The crime scene team has been through, but we want to preserve any evidence we might have missed."

The group expressed their understanding as they followed the chief up the front walkway. As they stepped inside, a heavy silence enveloped them. The house smelled of lemon cleaning products and something else – a metallic tang that made Angie's stomach turn.

"The kitchen's this way," Chief Martin said, leading them through a tidy living room. Family photos lined the walls, showing Frank and Kris in happier times. Angie felt a wave of sadness wash over her, so strong it almost brought tears to her eyes.

Courtney paused by one of the photos, studying it intently. It showed Frank Sleet, with his arms around a smiling Kris, standing in front of what looked like a university building. "They look so happy," she murmured. "It's hard to believe how quickly things can change."

Ellie placed a comforting hand on her sister's shoulder. "That's why we're here," she said softly, "to find out what happened and bring some peace to Kris."

As they continued toward the kitchen, Mr. Finch suddenly stopped, his hand reaching out to steady himself against the wall. "Oh my," he whispered, his eyes widening.

"Mr. Finch?" Jenna asked, concerned. "What is it?"

Mr. Finch shook his head slightly, as if trying to clear it. "Just a flash," he said. "But ... there was anger here. And fear. A great deal of fear."

The kitchen was a different story altogether. Despite the crime scene team's efforts, there were still signs of the violent act that had taken place. A large dark stain marred the otherwise spotless wood floor, surrounded by numbered evidence markers. Some of the drawers and cabinets stood open, their contents in disarray.

"This is where Mrs. Moran-Sleet found her husband," Chief Martin explained, gesturing to the stained area. "The body's been removed, of course, but this is where he fell."

Courtney stepped forward, her eyes scanning the room intently. She moved slowly, occasionally reaching out as if to touch something, then pulling back at the last moment. The others watched in silence, knowing better than to interrupt her when she was like this.

Suddenly, Courtney frowned. "Chief," she said, pointing to the counter, "was that book there when you first arrived?"

Chief Martin followed her gaze to a hardcover book sitting on the kitchen counter. "I ... I'm not sure," he admitted. "Why?"

"It feels out of place," Courtney explained. "Like it doesn't belong here." She closed her eyes for a moment, her forehead furrowing in concentration. "There's something else, too. A feeling of betrayal is in this room. It's strong."

Angie moved closer to the book, careful not to touch it. *The Catcher in the Rye*, she read aloud. "Wasn't that Frank Sleet's area of expertise? Twenti-eth-century American literature?"

Chief Martin said, "Yes, that's right, but why would the book give you a feeling of betrayal, Courtney?"

Courtney shook her head, frustrated. "I'm not sure. It's just a feeling, but it's powerful. It might have nothing at all to do with the book."

As Courtney spoke, Jenna gasped softly as cold air seemed to surround her. The others turned to her, recognizing the look on her face – she was seeing something they couldn't.

"Jenna?" Ellie prompted gently. "What is it?"

The young woman blinked rapidly, her gaze focused on a spot near the refrigerator. "There was ... I saw... I'm not sure. It was like a shadow but more solid. It disappeared so quickly, but I felt sensations of sadness, anger, and confusion. I think it was connected to what happened here."

Mr. Finch nodded thoughtfully. "The emotional imprint of the event, perhaps. It's not uncommon in cases like these."

As the group discussed Jenna's vision, Ellie found herself drawn to the kitchen table. She stared intently at a salt shaker, her concentration so intense that she didn't notice when it began to wobble slightly. Suddenly, it tipped over, rolling across the table and coming to rest against a napkin holder.

"Oh!" Ellie exclaimed, startled by her own unintended action initiated by her telekinesis. As she moved to right the salt shaker, something caught her eye. "Wait a minute..."

Carefully, she lifted the napkin holder. Underneath, partially hidden by the fallen salt shaker, was a small folded piece of paper. "Chief," she called, "there's something here."

Chief Martin quickly donned a pair of gloves and carefully unfolded the note. His eyebrows shot up as he read it. "Well, I'll be ... it seems to be a reference to the LeBlanc cold case. 'Where Karen fell, truth will rise.'" He looked up from the piece of paper. "What do you make of that?"

The sisters looked at each other and shrugged.

"The killer left it for law enforcement to find," Angie said. "First Lorrie Henderson shows up asking about the LeBlanc case, and now the killer mentions it in a note."

Before anyone could respond, Mr. Finch let out a long breath. He had been leaning against the kitchen counter, and now his eyes had taken on a distant, unfocused look that the sisters recognized all too well.

"Mr. Finch?" Angie said softly, placing a hand on his arm. "What do you see?"

Mr. Finch blinked slowly, coming back to himself. "I ... I saw him. For a moment, I saw the killer. Just flashes, mind you, but ... he was here, in this kitchen. He wore gloves and dark clothes. I couldn't tell if it was a man or a woman. I couldn't see the face, but I saw him placing those paper flowers. It was deliberate. Like a ritual."

The group fell silent, absorbing this new information. After a moment, Angie spoke up. "I have an idea. It might sound a bit odd, but, well, you know me."

She rummaged in her large purse, pulling out a small container. "I baked these cookies this morning. I put intention into them – for truth and clarity. I thought they might help us if we got stuck."

Angie had strong intuition and a special skill where she could put feeling or intention into what she baked – so if she put the intention of happiness into a baked good, then the person who ate it would feel happy for a little while.

Chief Martin looked skeptical, but the others knew better than to doubt Angie's abilities. They each took a cookie, and as they ate, a strange sensation swept over them. It was as if a fog had lifted from their minds, leaving everything sharper and clearer.

"The flowers," Courtney said suddenly. "We need to look at the flowers again."

Chief Martin retrieved the evidence bag containing the paper flowers. They were delicate things, folded with obvious skill and care. As

Courtney examined them, her eye picked up on subtle details the others had missed.

"Look here," she said, pointing to one of the flowers. "The folds aren't quite right. It's like there's something inside, distorting the shape."

Wearing gloves, the chief began to carefully unfold one of the flowers. As the last fold came undone, a tiny slip of paper fell out. Written on it in minuscule handwriting was a quote: "Two roads diverged in a yellow wood, and I— I took the one less traveled by, and that has made all the difference."

"Robert Frost," Mr. Finch murmured. "But what does it mean to the case?"

"It's a message from the attacker," Jenna pointed out. "Maybe about a choice the killer made?"

"Or a choice Frank Sleet made," Ellie added. "Something that led to ... this."

As they pondered this new clue, Chief Martin's radio crackled to life. He stepped away to answer it and returned a few moments later with a grim expression. "Mrs. Moran-Sleet is here to speak with us."

The group stepped outside to talk with her.

Kris Moran-Sleet was a petite woman with graying hair and red-rimmed eyes. She twisted a tissue in her hands as she spoke, her voice barely above a whisper. "I still can't believe this is happening. We moved here for a peaceful retirement. Frank was so looking forward to it."

"Mrs. Moran-Sleet," Angie said gently, "can you think of anyone who might have wanted to harm your husband?"

Kris shook her head. "No, everyone liked Frank. He was kind, generous... although..." She paused, frowning slightly. "There were a few concerning phone calls."

"Phone calls?" Chief Martin prompted.

"Yes, later at night sometimes, Frank would get calls and he'd go into his study to take them. He said it was just an old colleague, but ... he always seemed quiet afterward."

"Do you remember when these calls started?" Courtney asked, her intuition prickling.

Kris thought for a moment. "It was a couple of months ago, I think. Right around the time we decided to buy the house and move here."

Angie looked at her twin sister. Another piece of the puzzle, but where did it fit?

Jenna asked the woman a question. "There's a book on the kitchen counter. *The Catcher in the Rye.* Does it belong to you or your husband?"

"It was one of my husband's favorites. He must have been rereading it."

"Mrs. Moran-Sleet," Jenna said softly, "did your husband ever mention anyone named Karen LeBlanc?"

Kris's brow furrowed. "Karen LeBlanc? No, I don't think so. Should I know that name?"

"It's probably nothing," Chief Martin interjected smoothly. "Just following up on all possibilities."

"Wait," Kris said. "Karen LeBlanc. Was she the young woman who was killed in Sweet Cove many years ago?"

"Yes, she was."

"It was never solved, correct?"

"That's right," the chief told her.

"Frank told me he'd met Karen in a coffee shop while he was working at the university in the next town over. He didn't know her well at all, but he was shocked when he learned she'd been murdered." Kris narrowed her eyes. "Why do you bring her up?"

"Just covering all the bases," Chief Martin told her. "Thank you for your time, Mrs. Moran-Sleet. We'll be in touch if we need anything else."

As they wrapped up their visit to the crime scene, the sisters and Mr. Finch shared their thoughts with Chief Martin.

"There's definitely more going on here than a simple burglary gone wrong," Ellie said. "The note, the flowers, the quote... it all seems to point to something bigger."

"And don't forget the book," Courtney added. "I think it might be important somehow."

Chief Martin's expression was grave. "I agree. Let's meet later today to go over everything in detail. Maybe we can start to make sense of all this."

As they left the house, each one lost in their thoughts, a familiar figure across the street caught Angie's eye. Lorrie Henderson stood there watching them.

"Ms. Henderson," Angie called out, unable to keep a note of suspicion from her voice. "Out for an early morning walk?"

Lorrie approached them, her keen eyes taking in every detail. "I am. I like to get some steps in early in the day. I heard about what happened," she said. "Terrible business. What are you doing here?"

"We have some experience researching crimes and criminals," Angie told her. "We assist the police now and then on a volunteer basis."

"I don't suppose you could tell me anything about what went on in there? For my book, you understand."

Angie took a quick look at her sisters and Mr. Finch, a silent agreement passing between them. "I'm afraid we can't comment on an ongoing investigation," she said firmly.

Lorrie's eyes narrowed slightly. "Of course, I understand. It's just, well, given the similarities to the LeBlanc case, I thought perhaps..."

"Similarities?" Chief Martin interrupted, his voice sharp. "What similarities would those be, Ms. Henderson? And how would you know about them?"

Lorrie seemed to realize she'd said too much. "Oh, I mean just general things. Small town, mysterious circumstances ... you know how it is with these cases."

As they walked away, leaving a flustered Lorrie behind, Angie felt they might be missing something. The murder, the cold case, Lorrie's presence ... how did it fit together? Or maybe, it didn't.

"We need to look into this LeBlanc case," Jenna said as they reached their cars. "If there really are similarities, then we need to know what they are."

"I'll dig into the old files," Chief Martin promised. "In the meantime, be careful. Whoever did this is still out there."

As they climbed into their cars to head home,

Angie knew one thing for certain – with the murder, the paper flowers, hidden messages, and late-night phone calls, this was only the beginning of a complicated mystery.

A chill ran down Angie's arms. What or who would be next?

4

By the time the Roseland sisters had gathered in the library of their Victorian mansion, the sun had long since dipped below the horizon, painting the sky in deep purples and blues. Antique lamps shone a pretty light over the room, illuminating floor-to-ceiling bookshelves packed with volumes of all shapes and sizes.

Angie carefully balanced a tray of freshly baked snickerdoodle cookies and a steaming pot of coffee as she entered the room. The rich aroma of the coffee and baked goods mingled with the scent of the books, creating an atmosphere that was pleasant and warm.

"I thought we might need some fuel for our

investigation," she said, setting the tray down on a well-worn wood table.

Courtney looked up from her laptop, her eyes bright. "Thanks, sis. I've just started digging into the online archives of the Sweet Cove Gazette. There's a lot to go through." She reached over to pat Euclid, who was sitting in the chair next to her.

Jenna, curled up in a plush armchair by the window, nodded gratefully as she accepted a cup of coffee and a cookie. "I can't believe we're looking into a forty-year-old cold case."

Mr. Finch, settled in his favorite wingback chair with Circe on his lap, looked up from an old leather-bound book. "There's a lot to go through. Every piece of information may be of help in cases like these."

As the group settled in, Courtney began to share what she'd uncovered about Karen LeBlanc. "According to the articles I've found, Karen was twenty-nine when she came to Sweet Cove in June, forty years ago. She was a freelance journalist, supposedly working on a story about favorite New England seacoast towns for summer trips."

"Why do you say 'supposedly'?" Angie asked with interest.

Courtney stared at the laptop screen. "Her notes

were never found, and back then, the police questioned if that really was the story she was working on. They thought her story could have been the motive for her murder."

Euclid grumbled low and deep.

Mr. Finch said thoughtfully, "I read that some folks thought she might have uncovered something about one of the town's prominent families. Others believed it was related to some kind of criminal activity she'd stumbled upon."

As they continued to discuss Karen's life and the circumstances surrounding her death, Jenna suddenly said, "Oh." She was staring intently at Courtney's laptop screen, which displayed an old photograph of Karen LeBlanc.

"Jenna?" Ellie asked, concern evident in her voice. "What's wrong?"

Jenna's eyes were wide, her face pale. "I ... I see her. Karen. She's standing right there near the bookcase."

The others fell silent.

"What does she look like?" Angie asked softly.

Jenna's gaze remained fixed on a spot across the room. "Like she does in her photographs. She's young and pretty. Long dark hair, brown eyes. She's wearing jeans and a red shirt. She's also wearing a gold necklace. She's trying to tell me something, but I can't quite make it out." A second later, Jenna said, "She's gone now."

As they went back to their research, Angie suddenly sat up straight. "Wait a minute. I think I've found something." She pointed at an online newspaper clipping. "There's a mention here of a Frank Sleet. He was a graduate student at the time, and he's quoted in an article about Karen's death. He said he'd met her a few times at a local coffee shop."

"So Frank Sleet did know Karen LeBlanc," Ellie said slowly. "Interesting."

Before anyone could respond, the doorbell rang and the two cats jumped down and raced away to see who was at the door.

"It must be the chief." Ellie went to the front of the house to answer the bell, and in a few minutes, Chief Martin's deep voice echoed through the hallway before he appeared in the library doorway, looking weary but determined. His usually neat uniform was slightly rumpled, and there were dark circles under his eyes.

The cats followed the man into the room staying close by his side.

"Evening, all. I hope I'm not interrupting."

"Not at all, Chief," Angie said, gesturing for him

to take a seat. "We've been waiting for you. We've been doing some digging into the LeBlanc case. Have you found out anything new about Frank Sleet?"

Ellie poured a cup of coffee for him and Chief Martin sank into an offered chair with a grateful sigh. "As a matter of fact, I have. It seems Professor Sleet had quite an interesting past. After getting his Ph.D., he spent years working for a private research firm ... a think tank. He returned to academia about twenty years ago."

"Any idea what kind of research he was doing?" Courtney asked.

The chief shook his head. "Not yet."

"Chief," Jenna said hesitantly, "I don't know what it means, but I saw Karen LeBlanc's ghost earlier this evening. She seemed to be trying to tell me something, but I couldn't understand what she was trying to communicate."

To his credit, Chief Martin didn't bat an eye at this otherworldly information. He'd worked with the Roseland sisters, and their grandmother before them, long enough to know not to dismiss their unique abilities. "Maybe she'll come back?"

As the group shared more of their findings and theories, the pieces of the puzzle began to shift and rearrange in their minds. The connection between Karen LeBlanc and Frank Sleet, the think tank, the paper flowers - it all seemed to be pointing toward something more than they had initially imagined.

"You know," Ellie said thoughtfully, "we should really talk to some of the older residents in town, people who were here when Karen was murdered. They might remember details that never made it into the official reports."

The others nodded in agreement.

"Good idea," Chief Martin said. "I'll put together a list of potential people I can interview."

As the discussion continued, Mr. Finch suddenly sat up straight, his eyes wide. "Oh my," he breathed. "How could I have missed it?"

All eyes turned to him.

"Missed what, Mr. Finch?" Angie asked.

"The paper flowers," Mr. Finch said, his voice filled with excitement and a touch of apprehension. "They're not just a calling card. They're a message."

"A message?" Courtney repeated. "What do you mean?"

Mr. Finch's gaze was intense. "In the language of flowers, each bloom has meaning. I believe the flowers left at the crime scene are telling a story. A story of betrayal, of secrets long buried, and of vengeance."

A chill seemed to sweep through the room at his words. The warm atmosphere of moments ago had vanished, replaced by thick tension.

"So you're saying," Chief Martin said slowly, "that whoever killed Frank Sleet, and possibly Karen LeBlanc, is using these flowers to communicate?"

Mr. Finch ran his hand over Circe's soft fur. "Maybe not specifically with us, but to communicate a message about why Frank was murdered."

As the idea was sinking in, a sudden ring of the doorbell made them all jump. They shared wary glances, wondering who could be calling at this late hour.

Angie rose to answer it, with the others following close behind. When she opened the door, they found Lorrie Henderson standing on the porch, looking nervous.

The cats stared at the woman warily.

"I'm sorry to disturb you so late," Lorrie said, her eyes darting from face to face. "But I've discovered something about the LeBlanc case, something you might want to hear."

Angie narrowed her eyes. *Should they trust this*

woman who had appeared in town so suddenly, just as these old secrets were coming to light?

"Ms. Henderson," Chief Martin said, stepping forward. "Perhaps you'd better come inside and tell us what you've found."

As Lorrie stepped over the threshold, the tension in the air seemed to thicken.

Angie closed the door behind the woman, her mind racing. The comfortable evening of research and discussion had suddenly transformed into something more.

As they all made their way back down the hallway and settled in the library again, an awkward silence fell over the room. Lorrie stood near the doorway, clutching her ever-present notebook to her chest, while the others watched her with varying degrees of curiosity and suspicion.

"Well, Ms. Henderson," Chief Martin finally said, breaking the silence, "you said you've discovered something about the LeBlanc case. We're all ears."

Lorrie took a deep breath, her eyes darting around the room before settling on the chief. "I've been doing some digging," she began. "Interviews, old records, that sort of thing. I've found a possible connection that I don't think anyone has made before."

She paused, as if for dramatic effect, and Angie had to resist the urge to roll her eyes.

Courtney, ever the peacemaker, smiled encouragingly. "Go on," she said. "What's the connection?"

"Karen LeBlanc wasn't just a freelance journalist," Lorrie said, her voice dropping to almost a whisper. "I have the feeling she was working undercover. Maybe for a law enforcement agency."

Euclid flicked his tail.

Chief Martin stared at the woman. "That's a pretty big claim, Ms. Henderson. What makes you think so?"

Lorrie reached into her bag and pulled out a folder. "I have copies of some declassified documents. They don't spell it out explicitly, but if you read between the lines..." She handed the folder to the chief, who began to leaf through it, his expression growing more serious with each page.

"If this is true," Mr. Finch said slowly, "it could explain why her murder was never solved. If she was working for the FBI, they might have covered it up to protect an ongoing operation."

Jenna thought back to the ghost she'd seen earlier and recalled that the spirit of the young woman had seemed conflicted, like she wanted to tell them something but couldn't. Or shouldn't.

Before anyone could respond, Chief Martin held up a hand. "Ms. Henderson, these documents are certainly interesting, but they're far from conclusive. I'll need to verify the information and look into it further."

Lorrie said, "Of course, of course. I have more leads I can follow up on. I was hoping, well, I was hoping we might work together on this. I know you all have a reputation for solving difficult cases."

The sisters looked at one another and Angie could see the doubt in Ellie's eyes, the curiosity in Courtney's, and the caution in Jenna's. She knew they were all thinking the same thing: could they trust Lorrie Henderson?

Chief Martin stood. "Ms. Henderson, I'd like you to come to the station tomorrow afternoon. We need to go over those documents in detail. Thank you for bringing them to our attention. If you don't mind, we need to continue our discussion."

Ellie stepped over to the woman. "I'll walk you out."

A heavy silence fell over the room as they all absorbed this new information. The connection between the past and present seemed to be growing stronger by the minute, the web of mystery expanding and entangling them all.

Angie felt unease wash over her. Was Lorrie truly there to help, or did she have her own agenda?

When the grandfather clock in the hallway struck midnight, the chief stood. "I'd better get going. We'll talk tomorrow."

Angie walked with him to the foyer and closed the front door behind him. The house seemed unnaturally quiet, the earlier bustle of activity replaced by a tense stillness.

"Well," Ellie said, breaking the silence, "I guess we'd better get some sleep. Something tells me tomorrow is going to be a very long day."

Jenna left the house to go home, and as Angie climbed the stairs to her suite of rooms where her daughter and husband were sleeping, her mind whirled with all they had learned. A possible law enforcement connection to Karen's long-ago murder, the paper flowers - it was all starting to feel over-whelming.

With a sigh, she entered her suite and closed the door, ready to rest and prepare for the next day.

5

At the police station, Chief Martin led the sisters and Mr. Finch into a small conference room. They settled into chairs around the table while Mr. Finch remained standing, peering out the window at the now-bustling street outside.

"All right," Chief Martin began, spreading out a series of documents on the table. "I've had my team working through the night to verify these files that Ms. Henderson provided, and I have to say, it's looking like her claim doesn't have much merit."

Ellie asked, "So Karen LeBlanc wasn't working for some organization like the FBI?"

Chief Martin said, "That's our conclusion. According to these reports, someone was part of an undercover operation investigating organized crime along the New England coast, but it wasn't Karen."

Courtney said, "This town is hardly a hotbed of criminal activity."

"Sweet Cove probably wasn't the primary target, but something brought an undercover investigator here," the chief speculated.

Mr. Finch turned from the window, a thoughtful expression on his face. "Perhaps it wasn't what was happening in Sweet Cove, but who was here."

The others looked at him questioningly, and he continued. "Think about it. A small, quiet town would be the perfect place for someone involved in organized crime to lay low, wouldn't it?"

Chief Martin looked at the older man. "That's a good point, Mr. Finch, and it might explain why the FBI kept the operation under wraps. If they were tracking a high-level target, they wouldn't want to risk exposing the investigation."

As they continued to discuss the information, Angie's mind wandered to Lorrie Henderson. The writer had brought them some interesting information, but something still felt off about her sudden appearance in Sweet Cove. Did Lorrie deliberately try to lead them down the wrong path regarding Karen LeBlanc to send them on a wild goose chase? Angie wondered if she was just being paranoid.

"Chief," Angie asked, interrupting the ongoing discussion, "what do you make of Lorrie Henderson? Do you think we should trust her?"

Chief Martin sighed, rubbing his temples. "That's the million-dollar question, isn't it? On one hand, the information in these documents was important to check out and discard. On the other hand ... her timing is awfully convenient."

Jenna, who had been quiet, suddenly spoke up. "I think we need to be careful," she said softly. "When I see Karen's ghost, I sense conflict, like there's something she wants to tell us, but for some reason, she isn't able to."

The room fell silent as they all considered Jenna's words.

It was Courtney who finally said, "Maybe we should talk to Lorrie again. See what else she knows. But we keep our guard up, and we don't reveal everything we've discovered."

The others nodded in agreement. It was a delicate balance they were trying to strike - gathering information while protecting their own investigation.

As they were wrapping up their meeting, Jenna

suddenly went rigid in her chair, her eyes wide and unfocused. She was having another ghostly encounter.

"Jenna?" Angie said gently, placing a hand on her sister's arm. "What is it? What do you see?"

Jenna's voice was barely above a whisper when she spoke. "It's Karen again. She's trying to show me something. She's sharing a vision with me. It's a place. I see ... water. There's a dock and a small building. It looks old, abandoned."

Chief Martin suggested, "Could it be the old boathouse down by Miller's Point? It's been abandoned for years."

Jenna's body relaxed and her eyes began to focus again. "Yes, that could be it."

Excitement rippled through the group.

"We need to check out that boathouse," Ellie said, already standing up.

Chief Martin held up a hand. "Hold on now. We need to do this by the book. I'll get a search warrant for the boathouse. In the meantime, I want you all to be extra cautious. Whoever killed Frank Sleet might be watching us, and I don't want anyone taking unnecessary risks."

As they filed out of the police station, the sisters

huddled together on the sidewalk, speaking in low voices.

"What do you think?" Angie asked. "About Lorrie, I mean."

Ellie shrugged. "She shared information with us, but I don't think she's telling us everything."

Courtney said, "Maybe we should do some digging of our own. See what we can find out about her background."

Jenna, still looking a bit shaken from her ghostly encounter, spoke up. "I think that's a smart idea."

As they debated their next move, Mr. Finch rejoined them, having stayed behind to speak with Chief Martin. "Well," he said, his eyes dark from the seriousness of the situation, "it seems we have a complicated case to dive into, but this criminal probably has no idea we are on his trail."

Angie smiled. Despite the danger and uncertainty surrounding them, there was something gripping about unraveling a recent crime and a decades-old mystery.

"All right," she said, her voice filled with determination, "let's get to work. We've got information to find and a murderer to catch."

As they dispersed, each heading to their respective businesses to start the day, Angie thought about the pieces of the puzzle that were slowly coming together.

But one question still nagged at her: what was Lorrie Henderson's role in all of this? Was she an ally in their search for the truth, or was she playing a more sinister part?

Angie resolved to keep a close eye on the woman.

As she opened the door to her bakery, the scent of fresh bread and sweet pastries enveloped her, and Angie took a deep breath. Her manager Louisa was already hard at work with the morning baking. Chatting with her friend and employee, Angie joined in with the familiar opening tasks.

An hour later, the first customers of the day came into the shop.

Smiling, Angie pushed thoughts of murder and mystery to the back of her mind. For now, she had a business to run, but later, when the sun set and Sweet Cove grew quiet, she and her sisters would return to the case.

Somewhere out there, was a killer.

6

The afternoon sun slanted through the windows of Sweet Dreams Bake Shop, shining light over the display cases filled with tempting pastries and cakes. The scent of coffee and cinnamon floated in the air, creating an inviting atmosphere that had made Angie's shop a favorite gathering place in Sweet Cove.

Angie was wiping down the counter when the door opened and she looked up to see Lorrie Henderson stepping into the shop, her leather bag tucked over her shoulder as always. The true crime author's eyes darted around the bakery, taking in every detail with the keen observation of a writer always on the lookout for material.

"Good afternoon, Ms. Henderson," Angie

welcomed the woman with a friendly tone despite feeling cautious about her. "What can I get for you today?"

Lorrie approached the counter, a small smile on her face. "Just a coffee. And please, call me Lorrie."

As Angie prepared the coffee, she studied the woman out of the corner of her eye. The author seemed less tense than she had been during their previous encounters, but there was still an air of intensity about her that Angie couldn't quite figure out.

"Do you have time to sit for a bit?" Lorrie questioned, gesturing to a small table near the window. "I've been working most of the day, and I could use some company."

Angie looked slightly surprised. "I'd like that. It's slow right now in here. It's a good time to take a break."

They settled at the table, sunlight warming their faces as they sipped their coffees. For a moment, neither spoke, the silence broken only by the voices of other patrons and the distant bark of a dog outside.

Finally, Angie asked, "So, Lorrie, where are you from originally? Maybe you mentioned that before, but I don't remember."

Lorrie set down her cup, her fingers tracing the rim absently. "I grew up in Maine, but I've lived in New York City for years now. I have an apartment in Brooklyn. I bought it a long time ago." A small smile played on her lips. "It's amazing how much it's gone up in value. I've considered selling it and cashing in, but I have friends there, and anyway, where would I go? I like living in the city. It's my home now."

Angie thought how different city life was from the quiet charm of Sweet Cove. She and her sisters had grown up in Boston before they all moved to Sweet Cove when Angie inherited the Victorian mansion.

"What made you decide to write about cold cases and true crime? It seems like such a specific niche."

Lorrie's expression turned thoughtful, a hint of sadness creeping into her eyes. "When I was a graduate student, I wrote an article for the student publication about a cold case that happened at our university. I did some research and found a few things that had been overlooked by the police." Her voice took on a note of pride. "The story caused the police to take another look at the case. A year later, an arrest was made."

She paused, taking another sip of coffee before continuing. "I felt like I'd made a difference. It's a small thing, but helping to catch a criminal can bring peace to a loved one and justice to the victim. I was hooked after that."

Angie found herself nodding along, understanding the satisfaction of helping others find closure. It wasn't so different from what she and her sisters did, in a way.

"How did you pick Karen LeBlanc's case to work on next?" she asked, curiosity getting the better of her caution.

Lorrie's eyes lit up at the question. "Because I grew up in Maine, I'm a New Englander at heart. Karen was killed in New England. She was a writer, and so am I. I guess I felt connected to her in a few ways."

Angie lowered her voice. "Who do you think killed her?"

Lorrie shook her head, a rueful smile on her face. "I have some suspects in mind, but it's early on. I think it's bad luck to talk about potential suspects too early in my research. I need to keep an open mind and follow the threads. If I set my mind on someone early in the process, it closes me off to details and clues that might lead me in a different direction."

Angie was impressed by Lorrie's professional approach. "I understand. That makes a lot of sense."

As the afternoon wore on, their conversation drifted to lighter topics. They shared stories of their younger years, laughing over shared experiences despite the years and miles that separated their upbringings. Angie found herself opening up, telling Lorrie about the quirks and charms of Sweet Cove that had made it such a special place to live.

By the time Lorrie stood to leave, the shadows had lengthened across the bakery floor, and the first hints of dwindling light were touching the sky outside. Angie walked her to the door, feeling a sense of warmth toward the writer that she hadn't expected.

"Thank you for the coffee and conversation, Angie," Lorrie said, pausing at the threshold. "It's been lovely getting to know you better."

Angie smiled genuinely this time. "I enjoyed it. Stop by anytime."

As she watched Lorrie walk down the street, her leather bag again in hand, Angie felt her earlier skepticism begin to fade. Lorrie Henderson, it seemed, was more than just a true crime writer chasing a story. She was a woman driven by a genuine desire for justice and wasn't so different from Angie and her sisters.

Closing the door, Angie turned back to her bakery, her mind whirling with the afternoon's conversation. She had a lot to think about and even more to discuss with her sisters. As she began to clean up for the day, she had the feeling that the conversation with Lorrie had somehow shifted the landscape of their investigation.

What that meant for the case and for Sweet Cove remained to be seen, but one thing was certain - the mysteries surrounding Karen LeBlanc and Frank Sleet were far from over.

Angie had a feeling that Lorrie Henderson would play a crucial role in unraveling the cases, for better or for worse.

It was early evening when the Roseland sisters and Mr. Finch met Chief Martin at the old boathouse on Miller's Point. The point was a rugged piece of land that jutted out into the sea, offering a panoramic view of the restless Atlantic Ocean.

The boathouse itself was a weathered wooden structure that had seen better days. Once used to store boats and fishing equipment during the harsh New England winters, it now stood as a reminder of Sweet Cove's maritime past. Its faded red paint was peeling, revealing the gray wood underneath, and the roof sagged slightly in the middle, as if weary from years of battling coastal storms.

As they headed away from the small gravel parking area, their footsteps crunching softly, Angie filled the others in on her afternoon chat with Lorrie Henderson. The salty sea breeze ruffled their hair as they walked, carrying with it the distinct scent of the ocean.

"Maybe she'll actually be helpful with the cold case," Courtney mused, her voice hopeful.

Angie shook her head slightly, her expression cautious. "We still need to keep our guard up," she explained. "We can't fully trust her motives until we know her better, but today was a start at least."

The group nodded in agreement as they drew closer to the water's edge. Mr. Finch leaned on his cane and held on to Courtney's arm as the waves lapped gently against the rocky shore, creating a soothing backdrop to their investigation.

"What are we even looking for?" Ellie asked as they circled the boathouse, her eyes scanning the weathered structure.

Chief Martin, his face impassive, replied dryly, "Anything related to the case."

Ellie rolled her eyes at him, a hint of frustration in her voice. "Seriously. Are we looking for something specific?"

The chief's expression softened slightly, a small smile playing at the corners of his mouth. "Your guess is as good as mine. Walk around. Let your skills lead you. If you pick up on anything, we can discuss it when you're all finished looking around."

With that, the group dispersed, each focusing with their unique abilities as they examined the boathouse and its surroundings. A bit of creaking from the old wooden boards under their feet and the distant cry of seagulls were the only sounds that broke the evening stillness.

Angie ran her hand along the rough exterior of the boathouse, hoping to pick up on any lingering emotions or impressions. The wood was warm from the day's sun, but she felt nothing beyond the usual sense of age and abandonment that clung to forgotten places.

Jenna moved slowly around the perimeter, her eyes slightly unfocused as she tried to sense any spiritual presence, but the ghosts that usually came so easily to her remained stubbornly silent.

Courtney peered through a grimy window, squinting to make out the shadowy interior. Dust motes danced in the fading sunlight that managed to penetrate the dirty glass, but nothing caught her eye as particularly suspicious or out of place.

Ellie, meanwhile, concentrated on the area around the boathouse, looking for any signs of recent disturbance or hidden clues, but the ground seemed undisturbed, save for their own footprints in the loose sand and gravel.

As the minutes ticked by and the sun sank lower, a sense of unease began to settle over the group. The lengthening shadows seemed to reach for them like grasping fingers, and the gentle lapping of the waves took on a more menacing tone.

Mr. Finch, who had been examining the door to the boathouse, suddenly called out, "I say, does anyone else hear that?"

They all paused, straining their ears. For a moment, there was nothing but the usual sounds of the seaside evening. Then, faintly, they heard it - a soft, rhythmic thumping coming from inside the boathouse.

Chief Martin motioned for silence as he approached the door, his hand resting on his holstered gun. The others watched, holding their collective breath as he carefully tested the handle. Finding it unlocked, he slowly pushed the door open, wincing at the loud creak of rusty hinges.

The group peered into the gloomy interior, their hearts pounding. As their eyes adjusted to the dim light, they saw the source of the noise - a loose shutter on one of the windows, gently knocking against the wall in the sea breeze.

A collective sigh of relief went up from the group, followed by a few nervous chuckles.

"Is this a wild goose chase?" Jenna asked, voicing the thought that had been on all their minds.

"Could be," Courtney admitted, her earlier optimism fading. "I don't feel much of anything here."

"Maybe it's the wrong place," Angie suggested, trying to keep the disappointment out of her voice.

Chief Martin removed his hat and ran his hand over his hair, a gesture of frustration they'd seen many times before. "That could be," he conceded. "I'll do some research and try to find other boathouses in the area."

"Wait a second." Courtney moved closer to the loose shutter that had been beating out a rhythm. The young woman moved the shutter slightly, and noticed something on the wall. "Look here."

Someone had scratched words into the wall, but they were now faded and hard to read.

Courtney touched her finger to one of the words. "It says 'Frank and'...." The rest was too weathered to read.

The others bent close to try and make out the other faded words.

"This is a 'K,'" Jenna told them, "but the rest of the letters are too far gone."

"Frank and K?" Angie said. "Could it possibly be Frank Sleet who carved those words into the wall?"

"Frank isn't that unusual of a name," the chief pointed out.

"Could the K stand for Karen?" Ellie asked.

The chief shook his head. "It's too much of a stretch for us to glean any meaning from it."

As they made their way back to the parking area, the group's earlier anticipation had been replaced by a sense of discouragement. Long shadows moved across Miller's Point, as if mirroring their fading hopes of finding some relevant clues to the case.

"Don't lose heart," Mr. Finch said, his voice carrying a note of encouragement. "Remember, every investigation has its ups and downs. We may not have found what we were looking for today, but that doesn't mean we won't tomorrow."

The sisters nodded, grateful for the older man's wisdom and optimism. As they reached their cars, Chief Martin turned to address them one last time.

"Get some rest, all of you," he said, his tone gruff but caring. "We'll regroup and figure out our next move."

As they drove away from Miller's Point, the old boathouse disappeared into the gathering twilight, but even as it faded from view, the mystery it represented loomed larger than ever in their minds. The secrets of Karen LeBlanc and Frank Sleet were still out there, waiting to be uncovered, and the Roseland sisters and Mr. Finch were determined to find them, no matter how many dead ends they had to navigate along the way.

The drive back to Sweet Cove was quiet, each person lost in their own thoughts about the case. As the familiar streets of their hometown came into view, a sense of resolve began to replace their earlier disappointment. They may not have found what they were looking for at the boathouse, but tomorrow was another day, and with it would come new leads, new theories, and maybe, a few answers.

7

The bright October sun hung high in a cloudless sky, its warmth caressing the quaint coastal town of Sweet Cove. The Roseland family, along with Mr. Finch and his girlfriend Betty Hayes, had decided to take advantage of the unseasonably warm weather for a day at the beach. The long, white sand stretch of beach at the end of their street beckoned, promising a day of relaxation and fun.

Angie led the charge, her hair pulled back in a high ponytail and her oversized beach bag slung over one shoulder. "Come on, everyone," she called back to the group trailing behind her. "The tide's coming in, and I want to get a good spot."

Her husband Josh followed close behind, his hands carrying a couple of folding chairs. Earlier, they'd loaded Ellie's van with more lawn chairs, blankets, coolers, towels, and other supplies. "Angie, honey, the beach isn't going anywhere." He chuckled, adjusting his grip on the chairs.

Their daughter Gigi skipped alongside, her little feet kicking up puffs of sand with each step. "Daddy, can we build a sandcastle as big as our house?" she asked, her eyes wide with excitement.

Josh grinned down at her. "We can certainly try, pumpkin. Maybe we'll even add a moat."

"I can't wait to try surfing," Courtney exclaimed, her eyes sparkling with excitement as she carried a bright yellow surfboard under her arm. Her husband Rufus grinned, his own board tucked under his arm.

"Just remember, the waves here aren't quite like the ones back in Cornwall," Rufus teased, his British accent more pronounced in his excitement.

"Just don't forget about us landlubbers," Jenna teased, gesturing to herself and her husband Tom, who was pulling a wagon filled with beach toys and their daughter Libby's favorite inflatable dolphin.

Tom playfully flexed his bicep. "Landlubber? Speak for yourself. I'll have you know I was quite the beach volleyball champion back in the day."

Jenna raised an eyebrow skeptically. "Oh, really? And when exactly was this 'day' of yours?"

Ellie and Jack drove by in the van.

"We'll see who has the most fun out there," Ellie called out with a competitive grin. "I bet we can paddle circles around you surfers."

"Just watch out for the shark fins," Jack said with a wink.

Ellie playfully swatted his arm. "Don't even joke about that."

Mr. Finch and Betty strolled slowly along hand in hand.

"I must say, I'm looking forward to a bit of R&R," Mr. Finch said, adjusting his straw hat.

Betty smiled up at him. "Just promise me you won't overdo it, Victor. Remember what happened at the bowling alley last month."

Mr. Finch's cheeks reddened slightly. "My dear, I assure you, my back is fully recovered, and I've learned my lesson about attempting the 'Tornado Twist' bowling technique."

As they reached their chosen spot on the beach, everyone sprang into action. Blankets were spread, chairs unfolded, and umbrellas planted firmly in the sand. Within minutes, their little patch of paradise was set up.

"Last one in the water's a rotten egg," Jenna shouted, already racing toward the waves. Libby and Gigi were hot on her heels, both girls shrieking with delight as the cool water lapped at their feet.

"Girls, wait for us," Angie called out, hurriedly applying sunscreen to her arms. "Josh, can you—"

"On it," Josh replied, already jogging after the excited children, a bottle of kid-friendly sunscreen in hand.

Courtney and Rufus wasted no time in grabbing their surfboards and paddling out to catch the waves. From the shore, the others watched as they gracefully rode the swells, Courtney's laughter carrying across the water.

"Show-offs," Tom muttered good-naturedly, as Courtney executed a particularly impressive turn.

Jenna patted his arm consolingly. "Come on, beach volleyball champion. Let's show them what we can do with a board."

They opted for boogie boarding, riding the smaller waves closer to shore. Their shouts of excitement mingled with the girls' giggles, creating a joyful soundtrack to the day.

"Tom, watch out for that—" Jenna's warning came too late as a wave caught Tom off guard, flipping him head over heels. He emerged, spluttering and laughing, his hair plastered to his forehead.

"I meant to do that," he insisted, striking a pose that sent Jenna into fits of laughter.

Ellie and Jack prepared to launch their kayaks, but before they could, Mr. Finch surprised everyone by asking to join in.

"Victor, are you sure?" Betty asked with concern in her voice. "Remember, you're not as young as you used to be."

Mr. Finch drew himself up to his full height. "My dear, one is never too old for adventure," he replied with a twinkle in his eye. "Rufus, my boy, would you care to accompany an old man on his voyage?"

Rufus, who had just returned from his surfing session, grinned broadly. "It would be my honor, Mr. Finch. Just promise me you won't try any 'Tornado Twist' moves out there."

As they pushed off into the waves, Mr. Finch's initial trepidation gave way to unbridled joy. "Whee!" he squealed as they crested a particularly large wave, his normally composed demeanor forgotten in the thrill of the moment.

"I never thought I'd see the day," Betty mused, watching her boyfriend. "Victor Finch, daredevil kayaker."

Back on shore, Angie and Josh had set up a volleyball net. The soft thud of the ball and their good-natured trash talk added to the day's festive atmosphere.

"Angie, your serve is really getting better," Betty commented from her beach chair.

Angie grinned. "Thanks! I've been practicing. Though I think Josh has been letting me win."

Josh gasped in mock offense. "I would never. You wound me, madam."

As the afternoon wore on, hunger began to set in. Josh and Tom set about digging a fire pit, while Angie and Betty unpacked the food. The aroma of the grilling food soon filled the air, making everyone's mouths water.

"All right, troops," Angie called out. "Food's almost ready. Time to come in and dry off."

The group gathered around the long table they'd set up, laden with an array of delicious dishes. Hamburgers, hot dogs, and veggie burgers were piled high on platters. Bowls of crisp green salad, juicy fruit salad, creamy potato salad, and refreshing cucumber and tomato salad were passed around. Pitchers of lemonade and iced tea stood ready to quench their thirst.

"Angie, this potato salad is delicious," Ellie said around a mouthful. "You have to give me the recipe."

Angie smiled mysteriously. "Family secret, I'm afraid. Passed down from our great-grandmother."

"Oh, come on," Courtney chimed in. "We're family."

"Nice try." Angie laughed. "But a secret's a secret."

As they ate, the conversation flowed freely, punctuated by laughter and the occasional playful argument over who had caught the best wave or made the most impressive sandcastle.

"I'm so happy Mr. Finch went kayaking," Courtney said, shaking her head in admiration. "You've got some hidden talents, sir."

Mr. Finch puffed up his chest proudly. "Never underestimate the vitality of older people. Why, in my younger days, I once swam the English Channel."

Betty raised an eyebrow and joked. "Victor, wasn't that the time you fell off your friend's boat?"

The group erupted in laughter as Mr. Finch's cheeks reddened. "Well," he huffed, "it was a very rough crossing."

After the main course, Angie brought out a platter piled high with homemade cookies and a key

J. A. WHITING

lime pie. "And don't forget," she added with a grin, "we've got s'mores fixings for later."

"Mommy, can we roast marshmallows now?" Gigi asked, her eyes wide and pleading.

Angie laughed. "Let's let our food settle a bit first, sweetie. Why don't you and Libby start on the other sandcastle you were talking about?"

As the sun began its descent toward the horizon, the sky turned into brilliant streaks of oranges and pinks, and the group divided into teams for beach games.

Badminton rackets were wielded with varying degrees of skill, frisbees soared through the air, only occasionally landing where intended, and the satisfying thunks of beanbags hitting cornhole boards echoed across the beach.

"Ha! That's game point," Ellie crowed triumphantly as her beanbag sailed perfectly through the hole.

Jack groaned good-naturedly. "I demand a rematch. The sun was in my eyes."

"Excuses, excuses," Ellie teased, planting a kiss on his cheek.

As twilight settled in, they gathered around the fire pit. Gigi and Libby, worn out from the day's excitement, curled up on blankets, quickly drifting off to sleep despite the chatter around them.

"You know," Josh said, roasting a marshmallow for his s'more, "days like this remind me of when I was a kid. I remember that summer when my brother and I tried to build a raft to sail to a 'secret island.'"

Angie groaned, covering her face with her hands. "Oh no, not that story again."

But the others clamored to hear it, and soon Josh was regaling them with the tale of their ill-fated nautical adventure.

"So, there we were," he said, gesturing dramatically with his half-eaten s'more, "halfway across the cove on our 'raft' – which was really just a bunch of driftwood tied together with some jump ropes."

"I bet your brother still hasn't forgiven you for that," Angie interjected, though her eyes sparkled with amusement.

Josh continued, undeterred. "Then suddenly, we heard this loud crack. Next thing we know, we're all in the water, and our 'raft' is floating away in pieces."

The group laughed heartily, trying to imagine a young Josh and his brother floundering in the water.

"How did you get back to shore?" Rufus asked, wiping tears from his eyes.

Angie smirked. "Oh, that is the best part. Tell them, Josh."

Josh's cheeks reddened slightly. "Well, it turns out we weren't as far out as we thought. We could touch the bottom the whole time."

This revelation set off another round of laughter. As the chuckles died down, Jenna spoke up. "Oh, that reminds me of the time Tom and I tried to go stargazing."

And so, the tales from their youth continued - some embarrassing, some heartwarming, all of them cherished memories. The crackling fire, the sound of waves lapping at the shore, and the warm glow of friendship and family created a perfect end to a wonderful day.

As the first stars began to twinkle in the darkening sky, they knew it was time to head home. With a communal effort, they packed up their belongings, loaded the van, and took one last look at the peaceful beach.

"We should do this more often," Jenna said softly, leaning against Tom.

"It's probably our last beach day of this year but definitely next summer," Tom told her as he wrapped his arm around her waist.

There were murmurs of agreement from everyone. As they made their way back to the Victorian, sand in their hair and smiles on their faces, they all felt refreshed and reconnected.

Angie, bringing up the rear with a sleeping Gigi in her arms, couldn't help but feel a wave of contentment wash over her. These were the moments that made everything worthwhile - the laughter, the love, the simple joy of being together.

"Penny for your thoughts?" Josh asked, falling into step beside her.

Angie smiled up at him. "Just thinking how lucky we are. To have all this, to have each other."

Josh placed an arm around her shoulders. "We are lucky, and days like today... they're what it's all about, aren't they?"

As they reached the Victorian, the porch light welcoming them back, Angie made a silent promise. No matter how busy life got, no matter what challenges they faced, she would always make time for days like this - days of sun, surf, and family fun.

The group said their goodnights, each one heading off with sand in their shoes and joy in their hearts.

As Angie tucked Gigi into bed, the little girl stirred slightly.

"Mommy?" she mumbled sleepily. "Can we go to the beach again tomorrow?"

Angie chuckled softly, pressing a kiss to her daughter's forehead. "Not tomorrow, sweetie. But soon, I promise. Sweet dreams."

As she closed Gigi's door and made her way to her own room, Angie felt a deep sense of peace settle over her. Tomorrow would bring its challenges, but for now, she was content to bask in the glow of a perfect day with the people she loved most in the world.

8

Angie and Jenna Roseland sat at a corner table in the café of the Sweet Cove Resort, sipping coffee as they waited for Kris Moran-Sleet to join them. Kris was staying temporarily at the resort until the police were done processing the scene at the house. The sisters had chosen the neutral location for their interview, hoping it would put Frank Sleet's widow more at ease.

As they waited, Angie admired the resort's elegant yet comfortable atmosphere. Her husband, Josh, had done an excellent job overseeing the renovations, transforming the building into a haven of modern comfort with a touch of New England charm. The cafe, with its high ceilings and large windows overlooking the sea, was particularly impressive. Soft, nautical-themed artwork adorned the walls, and potted plants brought a touch of nature indoors. The scent of freshly baked pastries wafted from the nearby kitchen.

"Josh really outdid himself with this place," Jenna murmured, echoing Angie's thoughts. "It's hard to believe it's the same building we used to visit as kids."

A proud smile showed on her lips. "He has a real eye for this kind of thing. The bookings have been through the roof since the changes were completed."

Their conversation was interrupted as Jenna spotted their guest. "There she is," she said softly, nodding toward the entrance.

Kris Moran-Sleet walked in, her steps hesitant and her eyes rimmed with red. She looked smaller somehow, as if grief had physically diminished her. The sisters stood to greet her, their faces etched with sympathy.

"Mrs. Moran-Sleet, thank you for meeting with us," Angie said gently, gesturing for Kris to take a seat. "We want to offer our condolences once again. We can't imagine how difficult this must be for you."

Kris's hands clasped tightly in her lap. "Thank you," she replied, her voice barely above a whisper, "and please, call me Kris."

As they settled into their seats, a waiter appeared to take Kris's order. She requested a cup of chamomile tea, her voice trembling slightly. Angie noticed how Kris's fingers fidgeted with the edge of the tablecloth, a nervous habit that spoke volumes about her emotional state.

"How are you doing?" Jenna asked gently once the waiter had left. "We heard you're staying here at the resort for now."

Kris's gaze fixed on the table. "Yes, until the police are done processing the scene at the house. It seems I can return tomorrow, but I'm having a cleaning company come in and go through the place." She paused, taking a shaky breath. "I won't be able to live there anymore. I just can't. I'm going to put the house on the market as soon as I can. Once it sells, I'm going to stay with my sister in Boston for a month or two. I don't know what I'll do after that."

As Kris spoke, Angie observed the way her shoulders hunched slightly, as if she were trying to make herself smaller. There was a vulnerability in her posture that tugged at Angie's heartstrings.

"That seems like a good plan," Jenna said, her voice warm and reassuring. "It will give you time to process everything."

Angie's expression was compassionate but focused. "Kris, we know the police have already spoken with you several times, but we were hoping you might be willing to answer a few more questions. Sometimes people recall new details when they've talked about things a few times."

Kris's shoulders straightened slightly. "Of course. I understand there are follow-up questions that need to be discussed. What would you like to ask?"

Angie continued, "We understand Frank knew Karen LeBlanc when he was here in Sweet Cove about forty years ago. Could you tell us about that?"

A flicker of something - surprise? unease? - passed over Kris's face before she sighed. "Yes, Frank was doing some summer research at the university nearby. He met Karen at a coffee shop here in town, and they got to talking. They ran into each other sometimes at the coffee shop after that." Her voice grew softer. "Frank was devastated when he learned she'd been murdered. He didn't know her well at all, but it was still a shock to him."

Jenna nodded sympathetically. "That must have been terrible. We know that Karen was a journalist. Did Frank know what she was working on?"

"He told me it was a fluff piece about vacation

spots in New England," Kris replied. "She was doing it for a Boston newspaper."

Angie leaned in, her voice gentle but probing. "Did Karen ever tell Frank she was fearful of someone?"

Kris shook her head firmly. "Not to my knowledge. Years after it happened, Frank told me he'd known someone who had been killed. He didn't have much to say about it. He didn't know her well at all. We didn't talk about her except in passing."

Jenna took a sip of her coffee before asking, "And what about the phone calls Frank had received recently? Can you tell us about them?"

At this, Kris's shoulders slumped again. "I don't know who Frank was talking to. There were maybe five or six calls in all, sometimes later in the evening. Frank told me it was an old work colleague. He seemed very quiet and thoughtful after the calls."

"Did he seem concerned?" Angie pressed gently.

Kris paused, considering. "I don't think he was actually concerned. He seemed pensive. I worried the colleague might be offering Frank a job. I was hoping my husband didn't want to abandon our retirement plans. We'd just purchased the home here." Her voice cracked slightly. "I didn't press him about the calls. I figured he would talk about whatever it was eventually." She swallowed hard, her eyes filling with tears. "Our retirement plans are ruined now."

Jenna reached out, placing a comforting hand on Kris's arm. "I'm so sorry. This must be incredibly difficult for you."

After a moment, Jenna continued carefully, "Could Frank have been talking to someone else other than a colleague? Maybe he didn't want to tell you who it really was?"

Kris's eyes flashed, a spark of anger breaking through her grief. "We didn't keep secrets from each other."

Angie, sensing the tension, quickly stepped in. "So, Frank wasn't afraid of anyone?" she asked gently, trying not to upset Kris any further.

"No, he wasn't," Kris replied firmly. She took a long, deep breath, the annoyance seeming to drain out of her. "I don't know what I'm going to do without him."

"You need time," Angie told her softly, her voice full of compassion. "You need time to take care of yourself so you can think things through."

As the conversation lulled, Angie decided to shift gears slightly. "I hope you don't mind me asking, but how did you and Frank meet?"

For the first time since their meeting began, a small smile touched Kris's lips. "We met at a conference in Chicago. Frank was presenting a paper, and I was there representing my company. We ended up sitting next to each other at one of the luncheons." Her eyes took on a faraway look. "He made me laugh. Frank always had a way of finding humor in the most unexpected places."

As Kris spoke about her late husband, both Angie and Jenna noticed how her posture changed. She sat up straighter, her hands relaxing on the table. Despite the tragedy, the love Kris had for Frank seemed genuine.

"How long were you married?" Jenna asked gently.

"Thirty-five years," Kris replied, her voice soft with remembrance. "We had our challenges, like any couple, but..." She trailed off, her eyes filling with tears again.

Angie reached out, patting Kris's hand comfortingly. "It sounds like you had a wonderful life together."

Kris wiped at her eyes with a tissue. "We did. That's what makes this so hard. We were supposed to have so many more years with each other."

As their conversation wound down, Angie and

Jenna thanked Kris for her time and wished her well. They watched as she made her way out of the cafe, her steps slow and heavy with grief.

Once Kris was out of earshot, Jenna turned to Angie, her brow furrowed. "What do you think?"

Angie sighed, running a hand through her hair. "I'm not sure. She seems genuinely grief-stricken, but..."

"But there's something off," Jenna finished. "The way she reacted when we asked about the phone calls and the possibility of Frank keeping secrets touched a nerve."

Angie said, "Exactly. And Frank's connection to Karen LeBlanc ... was it really just a very casual acquaintance from forty years ago?"

Jenna added, "Or was it something more? Frank might have known more about Karen but didn't share that information with his wife."

As they left the resort, stepping out into the bright sunshine, both sisters pondered the meeting they'd had with Kris. The case was growing more complicated by the day, with each new piece of information raising more questions than it answered.

"We need to talk to the others," Angie said as

they walked toward their cars. "Compare notes, see if we can start connecting some of these dots."

Jenna agreed, her expression thoughtful. "It's time we did some digging into Frank Sleet's past. His work at that think tank, his academic career ... there might be something there that could shed light on his murder."

As they parted ways, each heading to their respective businesses for the day, Angie knew the truth was out there, hidden in the tangled web of past and present, of secrets and lies.

Angie opened the door and stepped inside her bake shop, the familiar scents of sugar and cinnamon enveloping her. For a moment, she let herself be comforted by the normalcy of it all, but as she slipped her apron over her head and began preparing for the day's baking, her mind was already racing, trying to piece together the puzzle that had fallen into their laps.

Frank Sleet, Karen LeBlanc, mysterious phone calls, and paper flowers... somehow, was it all connected?

As Angie kneaded dough for bread, she found herself reflecting on the interview with Kris. There was grief there, but there were also moments - fleeting expressions, hesitations in speech - that hinted at something else. Was Kris hiding something? Or was she simply a woman struggling to come to terms with an unimaginable loss?

The questions swirled in Angie's mind, like the flour dust in the air of her bakery's backroom. She knew that somewhere in the tangle of facts and emotions, they would find the answers they needed.

9

The grand Victorian house owned by Liza and Putnam Brewster sat perched atop a small hill over-looking the Atlantic Ocean. Angie and Courtney stood for a moment at the foot of the long, winding driveway, taking in the breathtaking view. The house itself was a masterpiece of 19th-century architecture, its pale yellow exterior was adorned with intricate white trim and a wrap-around porch that seemed to invite relaxing on lazy summer afternoons.

The beautifully landscaped grounds were a riot of color with carefully tended flower beds bursting with early October blooms. A winding stone path led through a small herb garden, the fragrant scents of rosemary and lavender carried on the sea breeze.

Old oak trees provided dappled shade, their branches swaying gently in the coastal wind.

"It's like something out of a storybook," Courtney murmured, her eyes taking in every detail.

Angie nodded. "No wonder the Brewsters' B&B is so popular. Who wouldn't want to stay here right on the coast?"

As they made their way up the driveway, the front door opened and Putnam and Liza stepped out. In their seventies, the couple radiated energy and warmth. Putnam, tall and lean with a shock of white hair, stood with his arm around Liza, a petite woman with sparkling blue eyes and silver-blonde hair cut in layers around her face.

"Welcome, welcome!" Liza called out, waving them forward. "We're so glad you could come."

The sisters climbed the porch steps, exchanging greetings with the Brewsters. Putnam's handshake was firm, his smile genuine.

"Come on in," he said, ushering them inside. "We've got some refreshments set up in the sitting room."

The interior of the house was just as impressive as the exterior. Rich hardwood floors gleamed beneath their feet, and the walls were adorned with a mix of vintage photographs and local artwork. The sitting room, with its large bay window overlooking the ocean, was filled with comfortable furniture and shelves lined with books and knick-knacks collected over decades.

True to Putnam's word, a tray of lemonade and iced tea sat on a low table, accompanied by a plate of homemade cookies that made Angie's mouth water. As a baker herself, she could appreciate the care that had gone into them.

Once they were all settled, drinking glasses in hand, Liza smiled. "Now, what can we do for you? Chief Martin mentioned you were looking into some old history."

Courtney set her glass down. "Yes, we're trying to gather some information about Karen LeBlanc. We understand you knew her?"

Putnam's expression grew thoughtful. "Ah, yes. Karen. That was a terribly sad business, what happened to her. But tell me, what got you interested in a forty-year-old cold case?"

Angie said, "Well, we believe there might be a connection between Karen's case and some recent events in Sweet Cove."

Understanding dawned on the Brewsters' faces.

"You mean the murder of that professor," Liza

said softly. "Oh gosh, do you really think they could be connected after all this time?"

"It's possible," Courtney said carefully. "That's why we're trying to gather as much information as we can. We were hoping you might be able to tell us about your interactions with Karen."

Putnam settled back in his chair. "Well, let's see. We'd just started our B&B back then. How long has it been now, Liza?"

Liza smiled, reaching out to pat her husband's hand. "We've run our B&B for about forty years. We got married the year before we opened. My parents gave us the down payment to buy this house. It needed a lot of work back then."

"That's right," Putnam agreed and picked up the thread of the story. "Liza and I had saved a good amount of money and invested it in updating the Victorian. We hired some employees and went full steam ahead. We didn't know much about running a bed and breakfast, but we had energy and were willing to learn."

Liza chuckled. "We were just starting out and were so excited about the future. That's when Karen came into the picture. She interviewed us for the story she was writing for a Boston news outlet."

Putnam said, "We met with her a number of

times and showed her what running an inn was like. She was surprised at how much work went into it."

"We were surprised ourselves," Liza added with a laugh, but then her face grew somber. "Some parts of the story Karen was writing were never finished. She was killed before she could complete all of it."

A heavy silence fell over the room. Angie spoke, her voice gentle. "When you were with Karen, did she ever mention being afraid of something?"

Putnam shook his head. "She worried she wouldn't get the articles to the news outlet in time, but she never told us anything about feeling she was in mortal danger."

"Did she ever mention having another job to do?" Courtney asked, her tone casual but her eyes sharp.

Liza looked confused. "Another job? No, she didn't."

Putnam added, "I don't know how she could hold down two jobs. The researching and writing seemed to take up all of her time."

Angie made a mental note. "Did she talk about a boyfriend at all?"

Liza's expression softened. "She told me she had been dating someone for about a year, but I got the impression she wasn't crazy about the relationship.

Her work took her away a lot, so that probably impacted them."

"Did something ever seem off with Karen?" Angie pressed gently. "Did you notice that something didn't seem right?"

Putnam shook his head. "No, I didn't notice anything like that."

But Liza was quiet for a few seconds, her brow furrowed in thought. "I did," she said slowly. "The last day she talked with us, she was opening her bag to take out her notebook and tape recorder. A small notebook fell to the floor, and I reached for it. Karen practically ripped it out of my hand." Liza's eyes widened at the memory. "I was kind of shocked. Karen quickly apologized. She told me it was her diary, and she was very protective of it. She laughed while she shoved it back into her bag. She told me it would be very boring if anyone else read it, but I had the feeling what was inside that notebook was anything but boring."

Courtney asked, "What did the notebook look like?"

"It was small, leather. It was red," Liza said, shaking her head. "Karen sure didn't want anyone looking at that notebook."

Angie and Courtney shared a look. This could be the clue they'd been hoping for.

"Do you remember anything else about that day?" Angie asked. "Anything at all, no matter how small it might seem?"

Putnam scratched his chin thoughtfully. "You know, now that Liza mentions it, Karen did seem a bit on edge that day. I remember thinking she looked like she hadn't slept well."

Liza said, "Yes, and she kept looking out the window, almost like she was expecting someone, but when I asked if she was waiting for someone to join us, she just laughed it off."

The sisters absorbed this information, their minds racing. Could the red notebook have contained information related to Karen's death? And if so, where was it now?

As if reading their thoughts, Putnam leaned a bit closer to the sisters, his expression serious. "I don't know if this helps, but after Karen ... after what happened, the police searched her rental cottage. They never mentioned finding a red leather notebook."

Liza's face fell. "Oh, Putnam, you're right. I remember wondering about that at the time, but with everything else going on, I guess I forgot about it."

Angie was already coming up with new questions. "Mr. and Mrs. Brewster, you've been incredibly helpful. Just one more question, if you don't mind. Did Karen ever mention anyone by the name of Frank Sleet?"

The Brewsters looked at each other and Putnam shook his head. "No, I don't recall hearing that name. Do you, Liza?"

Liza thought for a moment before responding. "It doesn't sound familiar, but you know, Karen did mention meeting a young graduate student at the coffee shop in town. I don't remember his name, but she said he was doing summer research at the university."

"Oh, wait a minute," Putnam said. "Frank Sleet is the professor who was murdered in town, isn't he?"

"That's right. We wondered if Karen knew Frank," Courtney told them.

As the interview wound down, Angie thought the Brewsters seemed genuinely fond of Karen and upset by her untimely death.

Putnam stood up, stretching slightly. "Say, would you like a tour of the place? We've made quite a few changes since Karen's time, but the bones of the old house are still the same."

Angie and Courtney readily agreed, eager to see more of the beautiful property. As they followed the Brewsters through the house, Angie smiled at the way Putnam and Liza moved in sync with each other, finishing each other's sentences and antici-pating each other's movements. It was clear that their decades together had forged a deep bond.

The tour took them through elegantly appointed guest rooms, each with its own unique charm, and a spacious dining room where breakfast was served each morning. Liza proudly showed off her modern kitchen, where she baked fresh muffins and bread for their guests every day.

As they stepped out onto the back porch, Court-ney's jaw dropped at the view. The garden stretched out before them, a tapestry of colors leading down to the cliff's edge where the land met the sea.

"This is stunning," she breathed staring at the scene.

Putnam beamed with pride. "Liza's the one with the green thumb. She's created a little paradise out here."

Liza blushed at the compliment. "Oh, it's just a hobby, but I do love tending to the flowers. Would you like to see the rose garden? It came into its second bloom of the season a while ago, but the roses still look lovely."

As they wandered through the garden paths, Angie and Courtney enjoyed seeing the gorgeous roses and marveled at how much work went into the gardens. Back on the front porch, as they prepared to leave, Angie turned to the couple one last time. "Thank you so much for your time and your hospitality. You've given us a lot to think about."

Liza smiled at the sisters. "You're very welcome. I hope you find the answers you're looking for. Karen deserves justice, even after all these years."

As the sun begun its descent to the horizon, the sisters headed down the stone walkway.

"A red notebook," Courtney murmured as they made their way back to their car. "It could be important."

Angie's expression was thoughtful. "The fact that it wasn't found after her death means someone must have taken it."

As they drove back into town, the beautiful coastal scenery slipping by outside their windows, both sisters were lost in thought. The mystery of Karen LeBlanc's death seemed to grow with each new piece of information they uncovered ... and somewhere out there, perhaps hidden away for forty years, a small red notebook might hold the key to unlocking it all.

They pulled into the driveway of the Victorian mansion they called home as the warm glimmer of lights promised the comfort of family and the chance to share their news. As they climbed the porch steps, Angie knew they would need to tread carefully in the days ahead.

For now, though, there was dinner to be had, family to catch up with, and new information to discuss. The mystery of Karen LeBlanc and Frank Sleet's murders would wait for another day. But it wouldn't wait for long.

The past had a way of catching up with the present, and Angie had a feeling that this particular past was about to come crashing into their lives in ways they couldn't predict.

10

The warm, inviting aroma of Greek cuisine filled the Victorian mansion's spacious kitchen as the Roseland sisters, Jenna's husband, Tom, and Mr. Finch bustled about, preparing dinner together. The late afternoon was slowly slipping away, signaling the approach of evening. Inside, the kitchen was a hive of activity, filled with laughter, conversation, and the sizzle of food cooking on the stove.

Angie stood at the kitchen island, her hands covered in flour as she kneaded dough for homemade pita bread. Her hair was pulled back from her face, and a smudge of flour adorned her cheek. Next to her, Courtney was carefully layering sheets of phyllo dough for a batch of spanakopita, her eyes narrowed in concentration.

Ellie opened the oven door to check a dish of fragrant moussaka, the rich scent of ground lamb, eggplant, and spices drifting through the air. Jenna and Tom worked side by side, chopping vegetables for a colorful Greek salad.

Mr. Finch, ever handy in the kitchen, wore a crisp apron over his pressed white shirt as he meticulously arranged a platter of dolmades, the stuffed grape leaves nestled artfully among sprigs of fresh herbs.

At the kitchen table, Gigi and Libby sat side by side, their little faces scrunched in concentration as they colored in their coloring books. The girls' laughter punctuated the kitchen's symphony of sounds, adding a joyful melody to the busy atmosphere.

Perched atop the refrigerator, Euclid and Circe watched the proceedings with interest. Euclid's tail swished back and forth, his eyes following the movement in the kitchen, while Circe seemed content to doze, only occasionally opening one eye to survey the scene.

As the family worked, they shared stories about their day. Tom sliced tomatoes and spoke about his latest restoration project.

"You should see this Colonial I'm working on," he said, his eyes lighting up with excitement. "It's got the most beautiful original woodwork I've ever seen. We're being so careful to preserve every detail."

Ellie, wiping her hands on a dishtowel, chimed in with her own news. "Oh, speaking of houses, two of the affordable townhouses Jack and I are building will be ready soon. It's so exciting to see them coming together."

"That's wonderful, Ellie," Angie said warmly, pausing in her kneading to give her sister a proud smile. "You and Jack are doing such important work for the community."

Jenna, who had been quietly focused on her task, suddenly looked up, her eyes sparkling. "I've got some really interesting news, too," she said, a hint of excitement in her voice. "You know those gift bags they give to the actors who present at the Oscars?"

The others nodded with expressions of curiosity.

"Well," Jenna continued, barely containing her enthusiasm, "the person who creates those bags has shown interest in including one of my necklaces or bracelets in each actor's gift."

A chorus of excited exclamations filled the kitchen. Courtney rushed over to give her sister a hug, careful not to get phyllo dough on Jenna's clothes. "That's amazing!"

"It's a real long shot," Jenna cautioned, though her smile remained bright. "I know two other designers who were approached in previous years but didn't make the final cut. Still, even being considered is huge. It could really get my name out there in front of high-end clients."

"We have no doubt you'll dazzle them, Miss Jenna," Mr. Finch said, his eyes twinkling. "Your creations are truly works of art."

As the family continued to chat and work, Angie moved to the oven, sliding in a pan filled with rich batter. The yogurt cake she was baking for dessert, along with a chocolate cake she'd already made, would be the perfect sweet ending to their Greek feast.

The kitchen was warm and comfortable, filled with the kind of easy companionship that comes from years of shared history and love. Outside, the last rays of sunlight faded, giving way to the soft glow of twilight. The warm light from the kitchen windows spilled out onto the lawn, a beacon of home and family in the gathering dusk.

As the meal neared completion, the delicious

aromas intensified, making everyone's mouth water. Gigi and Libby, having finished their coloring, now hovered near the adults, their eyes wide.

"Can we help set the table?" Libby asked, eager to be involved.

"That's a wonderful idea," Jenna replied, smiling at her daughter. "Why don't you and Gigi go with Aunt Courtney to get the dining room ready?"

The girls scampered after Courtney as she led them to gather plates and silverware.

With the final touches being put on the dishes, the family began to move their feast to the dining room just as Josh, Rufus, and Jack came into the house from the side door.

"It smells great in here," Rufus told them.

"I'm starving," Josh reported.

"Rufus and I came home for dinner, but we have to go back to the office right after we eat," Jack said.

The large oak table, a family heirloom that had seen countless meals and celebrations, was soon laden with an array of colorful and delicious-smelling dishes.

The moussaka, its top golden and bubbling, took center stage, and around it, platters of spanakopita, dolmades, and Greek salad were artfully arranged. A basket of warm, freshly baked pita bread sat nearby ready to be dipped in smooth, garlicky tzatziki sauce. Olives, feta cheese, and grape leaves added pops of color and texture to the spread.

As everyone settled into their seats, the room was filled with the soft glow of candlelight and the warm chatter of family. Euclid and Circe, having abandoned their perch on the refrigerator, now wound their way between the legs of the chairs, hoping for a stray morsel to fall their way.

Mr. Finch, seated at the head of the table, raised his glass. "To family," he said, his voice warm with affection, "and to new adventures. May Jenna's jewelry dazzle Hollywood, may Tom's restoration bring history to life, may Ellie and Jack's townhouses provide homes for those in need, and may we all continue to support and love one another through whatever challenges life may bring."

A chorus of "Hear, hear!" rang out as glasses clinked together. As they began to pass dishes around, filling their plates with the tasty food, the dining room was filled with the happy sounds of a family enjoying each other's company.

Conversation flowed, punctuated by laughter and the occasional "Mmm!" of appreciation for the food. The sisters shared knowing glances, silently acknowledging the joy of these moments amidst the mystery that had been occupying their thoughts.

As the meal progressed, talk inevitably turned to the case that had been consuming so much of their attention lately.

"Any new leads on the Frank Sleet case?" Tom asked, reaching for another piece of pita bread.

"We're still piecing things together," Angie said carefully, mindful of the little ears at the table. "Courtney and I are planning to do some more research later tonight."

"I'd help you, but I have to finish packing up some orders," Jenna said, a hint of concern in her voice. "Don't stay up too late. You both need your rest."

"We won't," Courtney assured her, though the determined glint in her eye didn't match her words.

The other two amateur sleuths in the family couldn't help with the research since Ellie had to prepare some rooms for B&B guests who were arriving the next day, and Mr. Finch was working at the art gallery after dinner.

As the main course wound down, Angie excused herself to retrieve the cakes from the kitchen. She returned moments later, carrying a yogurt cake and a decadent chocolate cake adorned with fresh berries and a dusting of powdered sugar.

"Ooh, cakes!" Gigi exclaimed, her eyes wide with delight.

The family laughed, the simple joy of a child's excitement for dessert momentarily pushing away the weightier concerns that had been occupying the adults' minds.

As Angie began to slice and serve the cake, she looked around the table at her family. Despite the mystery hanging over Sweet Cove, moments like these reminded her of what was truly important.

The warmth of family, the joy of shared meals, the laughter of children – were the things worth protecting. As the evening meal drew to a close, with bellies full and hearts warm, the family began to disperse. Hugs were exchanged, leftovers were packed away, and the dishes were cleaned up. The dining room which had been filled with so much conversation and laughter, gradually quieted.

Angie and Courtney finished tidying up. Once the house was settled for the night, they would reconvene in the family room. There was work to be done to unravel a mystery, but for now, they let themselves bask in the happiness of a family dinner, carrying the warmth of those moments with them as they prepared to dive back into the cold facts of the case.

The crackling fire in the family room of the Victorian sent a warm, flickering light across the homey space. Outside, the October wind whispered through the trees, occasionally rattling the windows, as if trying to join the sisters in their investigation. Angie and Courtney sat huddled over Courtney's laptop, their faces illuminated by the soft light of the screen.

Euclid and Circe were curled up on a nearby sofa, their fur gleaming in the firelight. Euclid's tail twitched occasionally in his sleep, while Circe's ears perked up at every creak and groan of the old house.

Angie had just returned from putting her daughter to bed, the faint scent of lavender baby lotion still clinging to her shirt. Josh was working upstairs in their suite of rooms, where the occasional rustle of papers punctuated the quiet of the space.

Courtney tucked a strand of hair behind her ear, her eyes focused intently on the laptop screen. "Rufus won't be home until late. He's going back to the law office with Jack," she murmured. "Looks like it's just us tonight to dig into Frank and Kris's backgrounds."

Angie pulled a soft throw blanket over her legs. "Let's start with Frank. What can you find?"

Courtney's fingers flew over the keyboard, the soft tapping a counterpoint to the crackling fire. "Here's a biography on the university website where Frank taught," she said after a moment. Clearing her throat, she began to read aloud, summarizing the information.

"Frank was a Professor Emeritus at the university in D.C. He did research during the summers of his graduate work at the university near Sweet Cove until he graduated with his PhD. He wrote his dissertation on similarities between the novels *The Catcher in the Rye* and *To Kill A Mockingbird*. He joined a think tank in Washington DC for about ten years before returning to academia, where he was a professor of twentieth-century literature. Frank worked at the university in D.C. for twenty years."

Angie asked, "Is there any information about the think tank? Can you find out what Frank was working on there?"

Courtney's fingers tapped away. "Here it is. They study and research international affairs and US foreign policy."

"I wonder why Frank left," Angie mused, absently stroking Circe, who had wandered over to curl up in her lap.

"Maybe he needed a change or just wanted to return to his interest in literature," Courtney remarked, reaching for her mug of green tea.

"You're probably right." Angie was quiet for a moment, her gaze drawn to the dancing flames in the fireplace. "What in the world did he do that got him killed?"

Courtney turned to her sister, her expression grave. "That's the million-dollar question."

Angie's fingers idly played with the fringe on her blanket. "The other question is: is Frank's murder connected somehow to Karen LeBlanc's murder?"

As if on cue, Euclid raised his head and let out a low growl, his big eyes gleaming in the firelight.

"Those phone calls Frank got at night might hold clues to his death," Courtney said, her voice barely above a whisper.

"The chief is looking into the calls, trying to find out where they originated," Angie replied.

Courtney set her mug down, a thoughtful expression on her face. "Was there forced entry into the house? I don't think I heard if the door was locked or not."

Angie shook her head. "The chief told me there was no forced entry, so Frank might have left the door unlocked since Kris would be returning from the grocery store."

"Or," Courtney offered, her voice low, "Frank knew his killer."

The sisters sat in silence for a minute, the only sounds the crackling fire and the soft purring of the cats.

"And what is it with these paper flowers?" Courtney questioned, breaking the silence. "Is the killer taunting the police? Is he or she just leaving a calling card? I don't get it."

"I don't get it either. Maybe they're communicating the story behind the killings, as Mr. Finch mentioned." Angie sighed, running a hand over her face. "Let's look at Kris's background next."

Courtney turned back to her laptop. Her fingers flew over the keyboard again, and in seconds, a biography of Kris's life appeared on the screen. "Kris graduated from Dartmouth's business school," Courtney summarized. "She worked as a hedge fund manager at several firms in DC. She was born in Maine and loved New England. It doesn't seem like they had any children."

"It probably wasn't Kris's background or contacts

that brought a killer to their house," Angie noted, her voice thoughtful.

Courtney continued scrolling. "Here's an article from a Maine local news outlet that did a human interest story on Kris. It mentions similar things that I read earlier. It does tell that when Kris and Frank decided to retire, they wanted to buy a home in Sweet Cove, a place they'd been to several times. They wanted the seacoast location and close proximity to Boston, so the popular town was a perfect choice."

"Unfortunately, it wasn't the perfect choice after all," Angie said softly, leaning back in her chair. "They were only here for about a month."

"What caused someone to hunt Frank down here in town?" Courtney wondered aloud, her voice filled with frustration. "Why not attack him in DC? He lived there for years."

"Something sparked a murderous impulse," Angie guessed, her eyes distant. "We need to find out what it was."

As the sisters continued their research, the night grew darker. The fire burned low sending long shadows across the room. Euclid and Circe had long since fallen into a deep sleep, their soft breathing a soothing backdrop to the tapping of keys and the occasional murmur of conversation.

Angie stood up to stretch, her joints popping slightly. She walked to the window, pulling back the heavy curtain to peer out into the darkness. The street lamps cast pools of golden light on the quiet street, and a thin mist was rolling in from the sea.

"You know," she said, turning back to Courtney, "I feel like there's something that's staring us right in the face, and we don't see it."

Courtney rubbed at her tired eyes. "I know what you mean. It's like some of the pieces are there, but we can't quite see how they fit together."

Angie returned to her seat, pulling the blanket back over her legs. "Maybe we need to approach this from a different angle. Instead of focusing on Frank and Kris, what if we dig deeper into Karen LeBlanc? There has to be a reason why her murder is suddenly relevant again after all these years."

"Good idea," Courtney agreed, her fingers poised over the keyboard. "Where should we start?"

"Let's see if we can find any articles about her work before she came to Sweet Cove," Angie suggested. "Maybe there's a clue in her previous assignments."

As Courtney began her search, Angie found her

gaze drawn back to the fireplace. The embers glowed softly, reminding her of the paper flowers found at the crime scene. What message was the killer trying to send? And why use such a delicate, beautiful medium for such a violent act?

The clock on the mantel chimed midnight, startling both sisters. They looked at each other with rueful smiles, realizing how caught up they'd become in their investigation.

"We should probably call it a night," Angie said reluctantly. "Fresh eyes in the morning might help us see something we're missing."

Courtney stifled a yawn. "You're right. I'm exhausted."

As they began to tidy up, closing tabs and shutting down the laptop, a sudden gust of wind rattled the windows. Both sisters jumped, then laughed at their own nervousness.

"This case is making us really jumpy," Courtney said, shaking her head.

Angie's face turned serious. "We need to be careful. Whoever killed Frank might not take kindly to us poking around in the past."

"I know," Courtney replied softly.

Yawning, the sisters made their way upstairs and wished each other goodnight.

In the family room, now dark save for the dying embers in the fireplace, Euclid's eyes gleamed in the darkness. He stretched languidly before settling back down next to Circe. Whatever secrets the night held, whatever dangers lurked in the shadows of Sweet Cove, the cats would be on guard, small sentinels protecting the family they loved.

11

The door of Sweet Dreams Bake Shop opened, and the wonderful aroma of freshly baked goods surrounded Chief Martin as he entered the bakery. The shop was quiet with only a few customers scattered here and there at the tables, sipping coffee and enjoying Angie's famous pastries.

Angie looked up from behind the counter, her face brightening at the sight of the chief. She quickly wiped her flour-dusted hands on her apron and reached for a clean plate.

"Chief. Good to see you," she called out warmly. "Have a seat. I've got just the thing for you."

Chief Martin's weary expression softened slightly as he settled into a chair at the counter. The lines around his eyes seemed deeper than usual from the long hours he'd been putting in on the case.

Angie bustled about. She sliced a generous piece from a pear frittata, the knife cutting smoothly through it. Steam rose from the warm filling, carrying with it the comforting scent of vanilla. She placed it on the plate and poured a cup of strong, black coffee into a mug adorned with pictures of colorful little cupcakes.

"Here you go," Angie said, setting the plate and coffee in front of him. "Just what the doctor ordered."

Chief Martin's eyes lit up at the sight of the frittata dessert.

"Angie, you're a lifesaver," he said, picking up his fork.

The young woman leaned against the counter, watching as the chief took his first bite. The look of blissful appreciation on his face was all the thanks she needed. After giving him a moment to enjoy the dessert, she broached the subject they both knew was on their minds.

"How are things going?" she asked gently.

Chief Martin sighed, setting down his fork. "I'm frustrated with the slow pace of the investigation," he admitted, his voice low. "We can't seem to find a motive for Professor Sleet's murder. It's like trying to drive down a street where there are potholes every few feet."

Angie nodded sympathetically. "It can't have been a robbery gone bad," she noted. "It had to be planned, what with the paper flowers and that note about truth rising where Karen fell."

The chief took a long sip of his coffee. "Exactly, but that just deepens the mystery. Why would the attacker go to all that trouble? What message is the killer trying to send?"

Angie was quiet for a few moments, listening to the soft clinking of cups and quiet murmur of conversation from the other patrons before returning to their serious discussion.

"Chief," she said finally, "were there paper flowers left next to Karen LeBlanc's body forty years ago?"

Chief Martin shook his head, a hint of frustration creeping into his voice. "I've been looking into that, but so far, there's no mention of paper flowers in the case notes, and unfortunately, some photos of the crime scene were ruined when the basement of the police station flooded years ago, so that's a dead end."

Angie's eyes widened in surprise. "Oh no, that's

terrible. What about newspaper accounts? Did they describe the crime scene?"

"We've read through the news reports from back then," the chief replied, taking another bite of pie. "There's nothing about paper flowers. It's like they appeared out of nowhere with this new case."

They chatted a little longer, with the chief savoring his pie and coffee as Angie occasionally stepped away to tend to other customers.

As the chief finished his pastry, Angie kept her voice low. "Courtney and I are planning to do some sleuthing into Karen's background," she confided. "I'm sure you've gone through everything, but two more pairs of eyes won't hurt."

A glimmer of hope showed in Chief Martin's tired eyes. "Please, look into the woman's life," he encouraged. "Don't hesitate thinking you're wasting your time because officers have already looked into Karen's background. You often find a detail others miss or dismiss."

Angie smiled, touched by the chief's faith in her and her sisters. "We'll do our best," she assured him.

A small smile tugged at the corners of the chief's mouth. "You always do."

As Chief Martin stood to leave, Angie wrapped

up a few extra slices of pie for him to take back to the station.

"Thanks for the pie," the chief said, pausing before turning for the door, "and for listening. Sometimes I think you Roseland sisters are the best detectives in Sweet Cove."

Angie laughed, a light blush coloring her cheeks. "We're just nosy, that's all, but we'll keep our eyes and ears open. Something's bound to turn up."

With the chief's departure, the door shut with a soft click, and Angie turned back to her work. The mysteries of Karen LeBlanc and Frank Sleet swirled in her thoughts like the steam rising from a freshly baked pie. There were connections to be made, clues to be uncovered, and somewhere in Sweet Cove, a killer to catch.

She glanced at the clock, noting that it was almost time to close up shop. Soon, she'd be heading into the house to meet with Courtney, ready to dive deeper into the past. As she began to clean up, wiping down counters and arranging the remaining pastries for the next day, she hoped they could find a nugget of information to move things forward.

The bakery slowly emptied as the last customers finished their treats and headed out into the cooling early evening air. Angie moved about, straightening chairs and sweeping floors, the routine tasks allowing her mind to wander over the details of the case.

Paper flowers, a murdered professor, a decades-old unsolved crime - how did it all fit together? And why now, after all these years, had the past come back to haunt them?

As she locked up the bakery and headed into the house, Angie took a deep breath, preparing to join Courtney in their investigation. She thought over the questions they wanted to ask and the connections they hoped to make.

As she stepped into the mansion's kitchen, Angie paused for a moment around the room. The scent of dinner cooking floated on the air. She could hear Courtney's voice from the family room, probably already setting up for their research session.

She straightened her shoulders, steeling herself for the evening ahead.

With a hint of a smile, she headed toward the family room, ready to dive into the mystery that had captured their town. The grandfather clock in the hallway chimed the hour, its deep, resonant tones echoing through the house. Another day was ending in Sweet Cove, but for Angie and Courtney, the real work was just beginning. The past and the present were about to collide, and the Roseland sisters would pick up the pieces and put them back together again, one clue at a time.

The family room was bathed in the warm light of the lamps, as Angie and Courtney huddled together on the plush sofa. The crackling fire added a comforting backdrop to their investigation, its dancing flames reflecting off the polished wood of the coffee table where their laptops sat.

Euclid was curled up in a nearby armchair, his tail twitching occasionally as if he too was deep in thought, while Circe prowled the perimeter of the room, her green eyes gleaming in the firelight as she kept watch over her human companions.

Angie tucked a strand of hair behind her ear as she scrolled through another webpage. "Okay, here's what we've got on Karen LeBlanc so far," she said, her voice soft in the quiet room. "She grew up in New Jersey and studied journalism in college."

Courtney's eyes scanned the screen. "Looks like she was pretty talented, too. It says here she worked for the college newspaper and even won an award from the school's journalism department for best story of the year."

Angie clicked through to another page. "After college, she worked at several different publications before moving to Boston. She landed a job at one of the smaller news outlets there."

"It seems she was a versatile writer," Courtney mused, reaching for her mug of black tea. "It says here she covered everything from human interest stories to sports and even did some more serious investigative pieces."

The sisters sat back, absorbing the information.

Courtney sighed, setting down her mug. "Basically, it's what the chief found out about Karen's life," she pointed out, a hint of disappointment in her voice.

Angie's eyes held a determined glint. "True, but sometimes it's not about finding new information. Sometimes it's about seeing the same information in a new light."

She turned back to her laptop, fingers moving over the keys as she initiated another search. After a few moments, her face lit up. "Oh, look at this," she said, turning the screen toward Courtney.

On the screen was an old newspaper photo, slightly grainy but clear enough to make out the

Sweet Paper Flowers

subjects. It showed Karen LeBlanc, looking young and energetic, standing next to a handsome man at what appeared to be a charity event.

"This is Karen and a man she was dating," Angie explained. "It's from a fundraiser for a food pantry. The caption says his name is Winthrop Kelly. This was taken about six months before Karen was killed."

Courtney studied the image. "They look happy together," she said softly, a note of sadness in her voice. "Poor Karen. Her life got cut short before she really had a chance to live it."

The sisters fell silent for a moment, considering Karen's tragic fate.

Euclid, sensing the shift in mood, let out a small grumble of concern, his eyes fixed on the women.

Suddenly, Courtney sat up straighter, her eyes widening. "I wonder what happened to Winthrop Kelly? I wonder if he still lives nearby? It might be helpful to talk to him."

She pulled her laptop nearer, her fingers tapping across the keyboard. After a few moments, Courtney's face lit up with excitement.

"Here he is," she announced. "He lives outside Boston. He owns a marketing and advertising company in the city." Her eyebrows rose as she read further. "And it seems he's done quite well for himself. The article mentions he's made millions."

"Let's contact him," Angie suggested, her voice filled with renewed energy. "Maybe he'd be willing to talk with us about Karen."

Courtney nodded enthusiastically, already searching for the man's contact information.

"Found it," she said after a moment. "Here's his business email."

Together, the sisters crafted a carefully worded email, explaining their connection to Sweet Cove and their interest in Karen's story. They were careful not to mention the recent murder or their suspicions about a connection, not wanting to scare off a potential source of information.

As Courtney hit *send*, both sisters let out a breath they hadn't known they'd been holding in.

"I hope he answers," Courtney said. "We need information if we're ever going to help crack this case."

Angie said, "We'll figure it out eventually. One way or another, we'll find the answers."

As if in agreement, Circe jumped up onto the sofa, wedging herself between the sisters and purring loudly. The simple act brought smiles to both the sisters' faces, a moment of normalcy in the midst of their increasingly difficult investigation.

Angie stretched, her muscles protesting after hours of hunching over her laptop. "We should probably call it a night," she said, glancing at the clock.

Courtney covered a yawn with her hand. "You're right. If I don't get some rest, tomorrow I'll fall asleep standing at the candy counter waiting on customers."

As they made their way upstairs, the old house dark around them, both sisters were lost in thought. They wished each other goodnight and quietly went to their suite of rooms.

In the family room, now dark save for the dying embers in the fireplace, Euclid and Circe curled up together on the warm hearth.

The next morning dawned bright and crisp, a perfect New England autumn day. Angie was up early, unable to sleep as her mind raced with questions about the case. She padded downstairs in her slippers, the smell of freshly brewed coffee leading her to the kitchen.

To her surprise, Courtney was already there, laptop open on the kitchen island and a half-empty mug of coffee at her elbow. She looked up as Angie entered, her eyes bright with excitement despite the early hour.

"He replied," Courtney said, turning the laptop so Angie could see.

Angie's eyes widened as she scanned the email from Winthrop Kelly. He had agreed to meet with them, expressing surprise and interest in their inquiry about Karen. He suggested meeting at his office in Boston later that week.

As the sisters began to plan their trip and discuss what questions to ask, the kitchen slowly came to life around them. The rest of the family began to trickle in, drawn by the smell of coffee and the promise of Angie's famous blueberry pancakes.

The mystery of Karen LeBlanc and Frank Sleet was far from solved, but with each passing day, and each new clue uncovered, Angie knew they were getting closer.

12

Angie wiped down the counters in her bakery, preparing to close for the day. The warm, comforting scent of cinnamon and apples still lingered in the air from the day's baking. Outside, the trees lining the street were just beginning to show hints of autumn colors, their leaves rustling gently in the warm breeze.

Angie looked up to see Lorrie Henderson stepping inside, and she noticed the true crime author seemed different today - her usual intense energy replaced by an air of weariness. Her shoulders were slightly slumped, and dark circles shadowed her eyes.

"Lorrie," Angie greeted warmly, setting aside her cleaning cloth. "Come on in. What can I get you?"

Lorrie managed a small smile. "Just a coffee, if it's not too late."

"Never too late for coffee," Angie assured her, moving to the coffee maker. "How about a slice of berry and custard pie to go with it? It's fresh from the oven."

As Lorrie nodded gratefully, Angie quickly prepared a plate and mug and brought them over to a table by the window, gesturing for Lorrie to join her. The late afternoon light streamed through the glass, warming the polished wood of the table and glinting off the silverware.

"How are you?" Angie asked gently as they settled into their seats.

Lorrie sighed, wrapping her hands around the steaming mug. "I'm exhausted today. I'm tired from working so much. This always happens when I'm researching. I throw myself into the work, and then I get so fatigued I can't think straight." She gave Angie a rueful smile. "I've been doing this for a long time. You'd think I'd learn to pace myself."

Angie said, "It's hard not to get carried away with work when you get immersed in it," she said. After a moment's hesitation, she added, "Have you found any clues you might share with the police?"

Lorrie's expression closed off slightly. "My

research and drafts of the story aren't ready for other eyes to see. They're preliminary accounts and may change radically by the time the book goes to the editor. I don't like to share information that's half-baked."

Angie tried another approach. "Have you inter-viewed people in the area who might know some-thing about Karen's murder?"

"Some," Lorrie replied cryptically, her gaze fixed on her coffee.

"We all might make quicker progress if we shared our information," Angie suggested gently.

Lorrie's voice was adamant when she responded. "I'm not ready to share more right now."

Recognizing the dead end, Angie changed tack. "Of all the books you've written on cold cases and true crime, do many of them lead to a resolution? Have killers been caught?"

Lorrie sipped her coffee before answering. "Only one, but in some cases, the books have caused police to reopen investigations. Hopefully, a few of those will lead to arrests."

Angie worked to process the information. She decided to lighten the conversation. "Have you had any time to see the sights around town?"

Lorrie shook her head. "Not really. I've just had

my nose to the grindstone. My days are full of research, talking to people, and writing. I haven't come up for air except to come here for an afternoon break and go to the grocery store."

"I never asked where your rental house is," Angie said. "You're close enough to walk here?"

A flicker of suspicion crossed Lorrie's face. "Yeah. Why do you ask where I'm living?"

Angie was quick to explain. "I can suggest a few things to do close by that won't take much of your time. It could give you a short break when you need it."

Lorrie relaxed slightly. "I'm about a half mile from here. I'm renting a place about a quarter of a mile from Frank Sleet's house."

Angie kept her tone casual. "There are nice places to visit within walking distance from where you're renting. The Sweet Cove Museum is one of the best of its size in the United States. There's also the section of town down by the harbor called Coveside where there are lots of shops, cafes, and restaurants. When you need a break, you could head down there."

Lorrie smiled, the first genuine smile Angie had seen from her that day. "Those sound like good places to see. Thanks."

"If you want any other recommendations, I'd be glad to add to the list." Angie got up to get the coffee pot and refilled the woman's mug before returning the pot to the coffee maker and coming back to sit at the table.

As they continued to chat, Angie asked, "How do you like the house you're renting?"

A flicker of worry passed over Lorrie's face.

"Is there something wrong with the house?"

Lorrie hesitated before responding. "The house is fine, but..." She trailed off, seeming unsure whether to continue.

"But?" Angie prompted softly.

With a long sigh, Lorrie explained, "I heard a noise last night when I was in bed. I keep my window open at night."

"What did you hear?"

"I thought I heard someone walk by my open window during the night," Lorrie finally said, her voice barely above a whisper.

"What did you hear exactly?" Angie asked, her concern growing.

"Movement. I don't know how to describe it, but something changed, like the moonlight coming through my window darkened. I thought I could hear soft footsteps."

"Could you have been dreaming?" Angie suggested gently.

Lorrie shook her head emphatically. "I wasn't dreaming. I woke up and lay there trying to go back to sleep, and that's when I heard it."

"What did you do? Did you get up to take a look?"

Lorrie's eyes dropped to the tabletop. "I didn't. I should have." She made eye contact with Angie again. "I was afraid to move. I just stayed perfectly still, listening. I heard footsteps moving away. I stayed still for about fifteen minutes, then I got up and shut and locked the window. It was unnerving. I didn't sleep the rest of the night."

Angie's forehead lined with concern. "Did you tell the police?"

"No," Lorrie admitted. "I felt stupid letting it get to me. Maybe I really was dreaming."

"It wouldn't hurt to tell Chief Martin," Angie suggested.

Lorrie shook her head. "It isn't necessary." She sat up straighter, clearly eager to change the subject.

As they continued to talk, an idea formed in Angie's mind. "My sisters and I and some of our friends are going out tonight. Want to come along? It might be good to get away from your work for a bit."

Lorrie looked surprised by the invitation. "Oh, no, I wouldn't want to intrude."

"You wouldn't be," Angie assured her. "It's a nice group. Everyone's friendly. Come along. You can always leave whenever you want."

Lorrie considered the offer. "Where are you all going?"

Angie's face lit up as she described their plans. "We're going to a nearby farm. There's a farm store, food trucks, drinks, and games. There's a huge lake, and they give boat rides. We're going to have dinner outside, play croquet, and then take a thirty-minute boat ride. They're going to serve ice cream on the ride."

A genuine smile spread across Lorrie's face. "Okay, you've convinced me. I'd like to join you."

As Angie gave her the details of where and when to meet, Lorrie narrowed her eyes playfully. "Just don't think I'll have a couple of glasses of beer and then spill all I know about Karen's murder."

Angie laughed, relieved to see Lorrie relaxing a bit. "Darn, you figured out why I wanted you to come."

As Lorrie left the bakery, Angie watched her go, a mix of emotions swirling inside her. She was glad Lorrie had agreed to join them - it would be good for the author to take a break from her intense work, but she wondered if there was more to Lorrie's story than she was letting on.

As she finished closing up the bakery, Angie thought over what she'd learned. The noise outside Lorrie's window, her reluctance to share information, her choice of rental location – did it all add up to something? She hoped that tonight's outing might provide some answers, or at least give her a better read on the mysterious author.

When Angie, her sisters, and their friends arrived at the farm, Lorrie Henderson's car pulled in just behind them, the author looking slightly nervous but excited as she stepped out to join the group.

Meadowbrook Farm spread out before them, a picturesque scene that seemed plucked from a postcard. Lush green lawns rolled gently down to a sparkling lake at the bottom of the hill, its surface glittering in the fading sunlight. To their left, extensive vegetable gardens showcased neat rows of early-autumn produce, while colorful flower beds added splashes of vibrant hues to the landscape.

The air was filled with a medley of enticing

aromas from the food trucks parked near the entrance, mingling with the sweet scent of fresh hay and blooming flowers. People's laughter echoed from the direction of a towering corn maze, its golden stalks swaying gently in the evening breeze.

"This is so beautiful," Lorrie breathed, her eyes wide as she took in the scene.

Angie smiled, glad to see the author relaxing already. "Wait until you see the view from the lake," she said, "but first, let's grab some dinner."

The group made their way to the cluster of food trucks, each offering a tempting array of local specialties. Jenna and Ellie headed straight for the truck known for its farm-fresh salads and sandwiches, while Courtney and Angie's friend Louisa, who managed the bakeshops, were drawn to the aroma of sizzling burgers.

Angie noticed Lorrie hesitating, looking a bit overwhelmed by the choices. "The fish tacos from that blue truck are amazing," she suggested gently. "Made with fish caught fresh this morning."

Lorrie's face lit up. "That sounds perfect, thanks."

Once everyone had their food, they gathered under a nearby pavilion close to the stage where a pop-rock group was playing. The wooden structure was adorned with twinkling fairy lights, creating a pleasant atmosphere as the daylight began to fade. The sisters' other friends, Sarah and Emma, joined them, completing their merry group.

As they ate, the conversation flowed easily, punctuated by laughter and exclamations of delight over the food. Angie watched Lorrie carefully, pleased to see the author gradually relaxing, even joining in with a few anecdotes of her own.

"So, Lorrie," Louisa asked between bites of her burger, "how are you finding Sweet Cove?"

Lorrie smiled, looking more at ease than Angie had ever seen her. "It's charming," she replied. "Everyone's been so welcoming, and the history here ... it's fascinating."

Angie caught the quick glance Lorrie shot her way, knowing they were both thinking of Karen LeBlanc and the case that had brought the author to town, but before the conversation could turn to heavier topics, Ellie chimed in.

"Who's up for some croquet after dinner?" she asked, gesturing to the neatly mowed croquet court visible just beyond the pavilion.

A chorus of agreement went up from the group. As they finished their meals and cleaned up, the sky had deepened to a rich indigo, with the first stars just beginning to twinkle overhead.

The farm had taken on a magical quality in the twilight, with lanterns placed along the paths and fireflies beginning to dance in the nearby fields.

The croquet game was a hilarious time with more laughter than serious competition. Lorrie, it turned out, had a wicked swing and a competitive streak that surprised them all. By the end of the third game, she was flushed with victory and grinning from ear to ear.

"I haven't had this much fun in ages," she admitted as they put away the mallets.

Courtney linked arms with her. "The night's not over yet," she said with a wink. "Wait until you see the gardens."

The group made their way down a winding path lined with solar-powered lanterns that cast a soft, ethereal light. The gardens were a riot of color and scent, even in the dim evening light, and the late-blooming flowers released their perfume into the night air.

As they strolled, Angie found herself walking beside Lorrie.

"This is amazing," the author said softly. "I can see why people fall in love with this town."

"Sweet Cove has a way of getting under your

skin," Angie agreed. "It's not just the beauty... it's the people and the sense of community."

Lorrie was quiet for a moment. "It makes what happened to Karen, and now to Frank, even more tragic," she said finally. "To have that peace shattered..."

Angie felt a pang of sympathy for the author. Despite her sometimes prickly exterior, it was clear that Lorrie cared deeply about the cases she wrote about. Before she could respond, however, Jenna called out from up ahead.

"Come on, slowpokes! The boat's about to leave!"

They hurried down to the lake where a charming pontoon boat was waiting at a small dock. The captain, a jolly man with a salt-and-pepper beard, welcomed them aboard with a hearty laugh.

As they settled into their seats, a young farm-hand appeared with a cooler full of homemade ice cream. "Choose your flavor, everyone," he said with a grin. "We've got vanilla bean, strawberry from our own fields, and maple walnut made with syrup from our own trees."

There were delighted exclamations as everyone made their choices. Angie opted for the strawberry, the sweet-tart flavor exploding on her tongue with the first bite. She noticed Lorrie savoring her maple walnut with closed eyes, a look of joy on her face.

The boat ride was magical as they glided across the mirror-smooth surface of the lake, and the captain pointed out constellations appearing in the darkening sky. The shoreline was dotted with the flickering lights of fireflies, and somewhere in the distance, a loon called hauntingly.

Angie felt completely relaxed for the first time in days. The mysteries of Karen LeBlanc and Frank Sleet seemed far away, replaced by the simple joy of a beautiful night spent with friends. She glanced at Lorrie, who was leaning on the railing, her face peaceful as she gazed out over the water.

As the boat docked and they disembarked, there was a general consensus that the evening had been perfect. They made their way back to the parking lot, the conversation flowing easily between all of them, Lorrie included.

"Thank you for inviting me," Lorrie said to Angie as they reached their cars. "I didn't realize how much I needed a night like this."

Angie smiled warmly. "I'm glad you came. We should do it again soon."

As they said their goodbyes and headed for home, Angie thought the evening had been more than just a fun outing; it had been a chance to see a different side of Lorrie Henderson. The guarded, intense author had shown a woman who could laugh, play, and simply enjoy the moment.

Driving home, with the windows down and the scent of night-blooming flowers drifting in, Angie found her mind drifting back to the case. She felt more certain than ever that Lorrie wasn't their enemy. The author might be keeping her cards close to her chest, but Angie sensed that her motives were genuine.

As they pulled into the driveway of the Victorian, she made a mental note to try again to collaborate with Lorrie. After tonight, she hoped the author might be more open to sharing information. Together, they might finally be able to unravel the mysteries that were hanging over Sweet Cove.

"It was a really nice night." Ellie parked the van next to the carriage house.

"Lorrie was fun. I'm glad we got to know her a little better," Courtney added.

Jenna said, "Maybe she'll be more comfortable around us now."

Angie could only hope.

13

The bustling streets of Boston's financial district surrounded Angie and Courtney as they made their way toward the towering glass and steel building that housed the Winthrop Group. The sisters walked briskly, their steps in sync, as they navigated the busy sidewalks. The city hummed with energy, so different from the quieter charm of Sweet Cove.

Sleek cars zipped by on the street while well-dressed professionals hurried past, their phones pressed to their ears. The aroma of coffee drifted from a nearby cafe, mingling with the urban scents of exhaust and hot asphalt. Despite the early hour, the city was already wide awake and in full motion.

As they approached their destination, Angie nudged Courtney. "There it is," she said, pointing to an impressive office building that seemed to touch the clouds. The building's facade gleamed in the morning sunlight, its windows reflecting the blue sky and puffy white clouds.

They entered the lobby, their heels clicking on the polished marble floor. A security guard directed them to the elevators, and soon they were whooshing upwards, their stomachs doing little flips as the numbers on the display climbed higher and higher.

The doors opened to reveal the offices of the Winthrop Group, and both sisters' eyes widened. The space was the epitome of elegance and success. Soft, plush carpets muffled their footsteps as they approached the reception desk. The walls were adorned with striking modern art pieces, while sleek furniture and state-of-the-art technology hinted at the company's forward-thinking approach.

A polite receptionist greeted them, and after a brief phone call, he ushered them toward Winthrop Kelly's private office. As the door opened, they were met by a tall, distinguished-looking man with graying hair. Seventy-year-old Winthrop Kelly looked fit and athletic, his handshake firm as he welcomed them inside.

"Please, have a seat," he said, gesturing to a pair

of comfortable chairs facing his impressive desk. The office, like the rest of the building, exuded an air of refined success. Floor-to-ceiling windows offered a breathtaking view of the Boston skyline, while shelves lined with awards and industry accolades spoke to Mr. Kelly's professional achievements.

Once they were settled, Angie began to explain their presence. "Mr. Kelly, thank you for meeting with us. As we mentioned in our email, we're here to discuss Karen LeBlanc. We do research for the police, and we're looking into her case."

Winthrop's expression turned serious. "I'm glad to hear the case has been reopened. I'd be happy to help in any way I can. It's been forty years since Karen died. I hope the police can find the person responsible."

Angie pulled out a small notebook. "Can you tell us about your relationship with Karen?"

A fond smile touched Winthrop's lips. "Karen and I dated for about a year or so. We met through mutual friends. We were both at the beginning of our careers. Karen was talented and dedicated. I'm certain she would have done great things if she'd lived."

"What was Karen like?" Courtney asked.

The smile on Winthrop's face grew wider. "She

was smart, involved, hard-working, and cared about people. She was also funny and optimistic. Karen was wonderful to be around. We had a lot of fun together."

Courtney shared a quick glance with Angie before asking, "Do you think you might have had a future together?"

Winthrop's expression turned thoughtful. "Initially, I hoped so, but I began to think it wasn't going to work out. Karen didn't want children, and I did. She was laser-focused on her work. It was everything to her. I could see I would always be second-fiddle to her. I didn't think there was room for me in her life."

"Had you broken off with her before she died?" Angie inquired gently.

"No, we were still together, but our time with each other was getting less and less. She traveled for her stories quite a bit, so we didn't see each other as much as we did at the beginning of our relationship."

"So you planned to break it off with her?" Courtney pressed.

Winthrop sighed. "I would have eventually, but at the time, I was still clinging to the hope we could be together." His eyes took on a faraway look, then he smiled softly. "A year after Karen's death, I met a wonderful woman. We married and had three children together. We have a beautiful life. I wish Karen had had the chance to live a long and fulfilling life."

Angie nodded sympathetically before shifting gears. "Did Karen ever mention being worried about her safety?"

Winthrop's eyebrows shot up in surprise. "She didn't express any concerns to me. Do you think it wasn't random? Was it a targeted attack?"

"The police are trying to determine that," Courtney explained carefully. Then, changing the subject slightly, she asked, "Do you recall Karen having a small red notebook?"

A chuckle escaped Winthrop. "I do. She always had that notebook with her. It was where she kept her notes on future projects and her to-do lists. She also used it as her diary."

"Did you ever read what she'd written in the notebook?" Angie asked, trying to keep her voice casual.

"No, I didn't. Karen was very private and protective of it." Winthrop smiled at the memory. "She said it would be bad luck for future stories if someone read her thoughts before she had a chance to work on them."

Angie leaned forward slightly. "At the time of her death, Karen was working on a piece for a Boston news outlet about New England summer towns. Do you think she might have been working on something else as well? Maybe a serious story that put her in harm's way?"

Winthrop's eyebrows knitted together as he considered the question. "It's a possibility. Karen was very involved in what she was working on – more so than what I thought was necessary for a light-hearted summer story. Maybe you're right - maybe she was investigating something that put her in danger. Whatever it might have been, she didn't confide in me about it."

As the interview wound down, Winthrop walked Angie and Courtney to the reception area. "Good luck with your research," he said earnestly. "I hope the police can find the person responsible for stealing Karen's life from her."

Once outside the building, Angie and Courtney found a quiet corner in a nearby park to discuss what they'd learned. The city continued to buzz around them, but there, surrounded by trees and flowerbeds, they found some moments of relative quiet.

"What do you think?" Courtney asked, her

voice low.

Angie sighed, pushing some strands of hair from her face. "I think Winthrop Kelly is genuinely sad about Karen's death, but I don't think he knows anything more than what he told us."

Courtney said, "But that bit about the red notebook ... that's interesting, isn't it? We know it wasn't found at the crime scene."

"Which probably means someone took it," Angie finished. "The question is, why? And who?"

They sat in silence for a moment, each one thinking. The red notebook, Karen's possible secret investigation, the connection to Frank Sleet's murder - it all swirled in their minds like pieces of paper in a windstorm.

"We should head back to Sweet Cove," Angie said finally. "I want to share what we've learned with the others. Maybe together we can start to make sense of all this."

As they made their way to the train station, the sisters thought about who might have killed Karen LeBlanc all those years ago. Did the same person murder Frank Sleet? If the sisters weren't careful, they might become the next targets.

The train ride back to Sweet Cove was quiet, and the scenery outside the window changed gradually from urban sprawl to rolling countryside, a visual representation of their journey from the fast-paced world of Boston back to their cozy seaside town.

As they neared Sweet Cove, Angie turned to Courtney. "You know," she said softly, "I can't help but think how different Karen's life could have been. She probably would have had a very successful career."

Courtney's eyes filled with sadness. "It's not fair, is it? To have your life cut short like that. It makes what we're doing even more important. We're not just solving a mystery - we're helping find justice for Karen and Frank."

The train pulled into the Sweet Cove station just as the sun was beginning to set, painting the sky in brilliant shades of orange and pink. As they stepped onto the platform, the familiar sights and sounds of their hometown greeted them. The salty tang of the sea air, the distant cry of seagulls, the friendly waves from neighbors - it all served to ground them.

They walked arm in arm down Main Street, where the shops and cafes were just beginning to light up for the evening.

"Let's gather everyone at the house tomorrow," Angie suggested as they neared the Victorian. "We need to pool our information and see if we can make some connections."

Courtney agreed, and as they climbed the porch steps, they both looked back at the quiet street for a moment. Somewhere out there, the truth was waiting to be uncovered.

14

The late afternoon sun created long shadows across the newly paved driveway as Ellie and Jack stepped out of their car. Before them stood a row of four neat, attractive townhouses, their fresh paint gleaming in the golden light. The couple's eyes, however, were fixed on the end unit - the first of their affordable housing project to near completion.

Ellie felt a surge of pride as she took in the sight. The townhouse was a perfect blend of modern design and classic New England charm, with its clean lines and warm, inviting color scheme.

"Ready to take a look inside?" Jack asked, a hint of excitement in his usually composed voice. His bow tie, as always, was perfectly straight, the opposite of the more casual clothes of the construction workers milling about.

Ellie nodded, her long hair catching the sunlight as she moved. "I can't believe we're finally at this stage," she said, her blue eyes sparkling with anticipation.

They made their way up the short path to the front door, the smell of fresh paint and new carpets greeting them as they stepped inside. The entryway opened up into a spacious living room, its large windows flooding the space with natural light.

"Oh, Jack," Ellie breathed, taking in the room. "It's even better than I imagined."

Jack smiled, clearly pleased with her reaction. "Let's go see the kitchen," he said, walking with her through an archway.

The kitchen was indeed impressive, with gleaming countertops and modern appliances that would make any home cook envious. Ellie ran her hand along the smooth surface of the island, imagining a family gathering around it for meals and conversation.

"It's beautiful. Let's go see the three bedrooms upstairs," she said, already moving towards the staircase.

Jack followed close behind. "And two full bathrooms. Just enough room to make sure it could comfortably accommodate a growing family."

They explored the upper floor, Ellie's excitement growing with each room they entered. The master bedroom was spacious, with an en suite bathroom that, while not luxurious, was well-appointed and practical.

Back downstairs, they checked out the full basement, discussing potential uses for the space. "It could be a great playroom for kids," Ellie mused, "or a home office for someone who works remotely."

As they stepped back outside, Jack pointed out the single-car garage and then gestured toward the expansive green space beyond the row of townhouses. "And over there," he said, "is the access point to the state park. I think that's going to be a huge selling point."

"Jack," Ellie said slowly, "I've been thinking about how we're going to choose the residents for these units."

Jack raised an eyebrow, curious. "What did you have in mind?"

"Well," Ellie began, "I was thinking we could do a lottery system. It would give everyone a fair chance, regardless of how quickly they can submit an application."

Jack looked thoughtful. "That's an interesting idea. We'd have to look into the legality of running a lottery, though. We have to make sure we're not breaking any housing laws."

Ellie thought about the practical considerations. "Of course, but if we can make it work, I think it could be a great way to ensure fairness and opportunity."

As the sun began to dip lower in the sky, Jack said, "We should probably head to dinner. How about that new place in Silver Cove?"

Ellie agreed, and soon they were driving the short distance to the neighboring town. Silver Cove, while similar in many ways to Sweet Cove, was slightly smaller and more rural. Their town had a more upscale feel with its marina full of sleek yachts and boutiques lining the main street.

The restaurant Jack had suggested was a popular Italian place, its warm lighting and rich aromas inviting them in from the cool evening air. As the hostess led them to their table, Ellie's gaze swept across the dining room, taking in the other patrons.

Suddenly, she froze, her hand gripping Jack's arm tightly. There, in a dark corner at the back of the restaurant, sat Kris Moran-Sleet and Lorrie Henderson, deep in conversation. The two women were leaning in close, their faces serious.

"Jack," Ellie whispered, nodding discreetly towards the corner. "Look who's here."

Jack's eyebrows rose in surprise as he spotted the unlikely pair. "Well, that's... interesting," he murmured.

Ellie felt a wave of unease wash over her. Something about seeing Kris and Lorrie together, talking so intently, set off alarm bells in her mind. Without quite knowing why, she knew they couldn't stay.

"Let's go somewhere else," she said quietly to Jack, already turning back toward the exit.

Jack, sensing her discomfort, nodded without question. They made their apologies to the confused hostess and slipped out of the restaurant, neither of them speaking until they were back in their car.

"What do you think that was about?" Jack asked as he started the engine.

Ellie shook her head. "I don't know, but it didn't feel right. Kris is supposed to be grieving her husband, and Lorrie ... well, she's supposedly here to investigate Karen's murder. Why would they be meeting like that?"

Jack pulled out onto the main road. "It does seem odd. We should tell the others."

"Definitely," Ellie said firmly. "We need to figure out what's going on. This case keeps getting more confusing by the day."

As they drove back to Sweet Cove, the sky darkening to a deep indigo, Ellie's mind raced. What connection could there be between Kris Moran-Sleet, the grieving widow, and Lorrie Henderson, the true crime author? And how did it all tie back to Karen LeBlanc's decades-old murder? Maybe Lorrie was interviewing Kris? But it seemed too soon after Frank's death to do that.

The lights of Sweet Cove came into view, twinkling like stars along the coastline, and in minutes, they pulled up in front of their house, a comforting sight after the unsettling encounter in Silver Cove. As they climbed the porch steps, Ellie could see the warm glow of lights in the family room, and when she stepped inside, she could hear the muffled sounds of her sisters' voices.

"I'll make some coffee," Jack said as they entered, understanding without words that it might be a long night of discussion.

Ellie moved toward the family room. Her sisters looked up as she entered, their faces curious at her earlier-than-expected return.

"We need to talk," Ellie said without preamble. "Something's going on."

As her sisters gathered around, their expressions full of concern, Ellie took a deep breath. Outside, the wind picked up, rustling the leaves of the old oak tree in the rear yard.

"We saw Kris Moran-Sleet and Lorrie Henderson in a restaurant huddled together at the back of the place. Something about it felt off."

They discussed possible reasons why the women had met and what they could have been talking about. After two hours of conversation without any resolution, the family members decided to leave it for another day, and they all headed off so they could go to bed.

The next day, the quaint seaside café buzzed with the gentle hum of conversation and the clinking of coffee cups as Ellie and Angie settled into a booth by the window. Outside, the late afternoon sun sent a pretty glow over the picturesque coastal town just twenty minutes north of Sweet Cove.

The sisters had arrived early, giving them a

moment to gather their thoughts before their meeting with Frank Sleet's younger brother, Rick. The café, with its nautical-themed decor and the smell of freshly baked pastries hanging in the air, was a cozy spot for what promised to be a difficult conversation.

"There he is," Ellie murmured, nodding toward the door.

Angie turned to see a tall man with a bit of extra weight around his middle entering the café. His brown hair was peppered with gray at the temples, giving him a distinguished look despite his casual attire. His eyes, sharp and observant, scanned the room before landing on the sisters.

As Rick approached their table, both Ellie and Angie stood to greet him.

"Mr. Sleet," Angie said, extending her hand, "thank you for meeting with us. I'm Angie Roseland, and this is my sister, Ellie."

Rick shook their hands, his grip firm but not overpowering. "Please, call me Rick," he said, his voice deep and slightly gravelly. "Frank was the more formal one in the family."

As they settled into their seats, a waitress appeared to take their orders. Once she had bustled away, promising to return shortly with their drinks, an awkward silence fell over the table.

Ellie broke it first, her voice gentle. "We want to offer our condolences for the loss of your brother. It's a terrible tragedy."

Rick's face softened, a flicker of pain crossing his features. "Thank you," he said quietly. "I loved my brother, but he spent most of his adult life in DC. We didn't really know each other well anymore. We'd often get together for holidays, but it's such a short time to spend with one another."

He paused, his gaze drifting to the window where the sun was slowly sinking toward the horizon. "We were hoping to connect more frequently now that he and Kris had moved to Sweet Cove." He shook his head. "I can't believe what happened to him. The police told me they believe it was targeted, not random. What in the world did my brother do to deserve being murdered?"

The raw pain in Rick's voice hung in the air, and Ellie felt sad for the man. "Your brother didn't deserve to die that way," she said firmly. "We're researching and interviewing people to gather as much knowledge about Frank's life as we can. The police are determined to bring the perpetrator to justice."

Rick's eyes glistened with a few unshed tears. The waitress returned with their drinks, providing a momentary distraction. As she walked away, Angie's voice was gentle but focused when she asked, "Can you tell us about when Frank was working summers in Sweet Cove during his PhD studies?"

Rick took a sip of his coffee before responding. "Frank was doing his doctorate in American literature. He worked at a nearby university for two summers doing research. After he graduated, he ended up working at a think tank in DC for a number of years. Eventually, he made his way back to teaching."

Angie made a mental note. "And he met Karen LeBlanc during one of those summers during graduate school?"

Rick blinked, surprise evident on his face. "The police asked me about Karen, too. Is there some sort of link between her cold case and my brother's death?"

"The police are still working on that possibility," Angie explained carefully.

"Karen died about forty years ago," Rick said, his brow furrowed in confusion. "How could there be a link between her murder and Frank's?"

Ellie stepped in, her voice gentle. "The police don't share all their information with us so we're not able to answer your question."

Angie tried to steer the conversation back to Karen. "Frank met Karen at a coffee shop?"

"Yeah, that's what he told me," Rick confirmed.

"Was he interested in Karen romantically?" Angie pressed.

Rick shrugged. "I'd say he probably was, but Karen was seeing someone else."

"How did your brother describe Karen?"

A small smile touched Rick's lips, as if remembering a long-ago conversation. "He thought she was smart, interesting, and lively. He liked how ambitious she was."

"Did he try to convince her to date him?" Angie asked.

Rick shook his head. "Frank enjoyed talking with Karen, but I don't think he was pressuring her. I believe he was respectful about her relationship with her boyfriend."

Ellie spoke softly, "Frank must have been very upset when he learned she was killed."

"He was," Rick said, his voice barely above a whisper. "He was devastated. He told me he'd just seen Karen that afternoon."

Angie asked, "Did Karen ever mention being worried about someone?"

"Frank never told me anything like that."

"Did he suspect anyone of her murder?"

Rick shook his head again. "He didn't tell me that he suspected someone. He really didn't know Karen that well. They'd run into each other at the coffee shop and would chat."

Angie paused for a moment, considering her next question. "Karen had a small red leather notebook that she had with her most of the time," she said. "Did Frank tell you about it?"

"No, he didn't," Rick replied, looking slightly puzzled.

"Did Frank tell you why Karen was in Sweet Cove?"

Rick took a long swallow of his coffee before answering. "Frank said Karen was supposedly working on an article about summer vacation places, but he wondered if it was something else because she didn't seem to know much about other resort towns nearby." He shrugged, the gesture conveying his uncertainty.

"Maybe it was early in her research of seacoast towns," Ellie suggested.

Angie made eye contact with Rick and spoke in a low voice. "Did Frank tell you he was concerned about anyone? Did he move away from DC because he was worried about something that might be going on down there?"

Rick shook his head again as he considered the question. "Frank seemed excited about the move," he said finally. "He didn't confide any worries to me."

Ellie decided to try a different approach. "Kris reported that Frank received a few phone calls from an old colleague right before they moved to Sweet Cove," she said. "She worried the colleague was trying to lure Frank into a teaching job."

A look of understanding crossed Rick's face. "Frank didn't tell me about any job, but I wouldn't be surprised if he'd joined the faculty of a college around here. Frank liked to be active and engaged. Maybe he was hoping for a part-time position somewhere as he transitioned to retirement."

The conversation continued for about fifteen more minutes, with the sisters probing gently for any additional information Rick might have. As the sun began to set, they thanked Rick for his time and assured him that the police would contact him with any news about the investigation.

As Rick left, his shoulders slightly slumped under the weight of his grief, Ellie and Angie remained at the table, lost in thought. The café had grown quieter. The dinner rush not yet started, and the soft strains of jazz music filled the air.

"What did you think?" Ellie asked, breaking the silence. "We didn't get much from him."

Angie's gaze fixed on the darkening sky outside. "No, we didn't, but it was worth talking with him." She turned back to her sister, her eyes thoughtful. "Frank's wife and brother both told us Frank didn't seem to be worried or concerned about anything. Was Frank hiding things from them? Was he keeping secrets? What was going on that got him killed?"

Ellie sighed, pushing her hair over her shoulder. "It's like we're trying to put a torn-up photo together, and the picture keeps changing."

They sat in silence for a moment, each lost in their own thoughts. The connection between Frank Sleet and Karen LeBlanc, the mysterious phone calls, the red notebook - how did it all fit together?

As they gathered their things to leave, Angie paused, her hand on her purse. "Are we missing something obvious?" she asked slowly, "Something that's right in front of us?"

Ellie said, "I know what you mean. It's like we can't quite see how everything fits together."

They stepped out into the cool evening air, the

street lamps flickering to life around them. The sound of waves crashing against the nearby shore provided a soothing sound to their troubled thoughts.

As they drove back toward Sweet Cove, the darkening sky above them mirrored the mystery that seemed to deepen with each passing day.

Tomorrow would bring new leads to follow, but for tonight, they would sit with their family, share what they had learned, and get ready for whatever secrets the coming days might bring.

15

The soft light of the setting sun filtered through the windows of the Victorian mansion's sunroom where the four Roseland sisters - Ellie, Jenna, Angie, and Courtney - sat around a small square table hunched over a jigsaw puzzle, their fingers working to fit pieces together. Mr. Finch sat in an easy chair, reading a book.

Euclid and Circe lounged nearby, their eyes half-closed in contentment. The peaceful scene disguised the serious conversation taking place among them.

"I always feel like we're missing something," Angie said, fitting a sky-blue puzzle piece into place. "Frank Sleet's murder ... how is it connected to Karen's cold case? Or is it connected at all?"

Ellie sighed, trying to fit another piece into the puzzle picture. "That's the big question, isn't it? We have no real suspects in Frank's case, and the connection to Karen is shaky at best."

Jenna studied the puzzle pieces before her. "Maybe we're looking at this all wrong. What if the cases aren't connected at all? Maybe the killer is toying with the police? Is it just a coincidence that Karen's murder was mentioned at the crime scene?"

Mr. Finch looked up from his book. "In my experience, there's rarely such a thing as coincidence in matters like these."

Courtney leaned back in her chair, stretching her arms above her head. "But what's the connection? Frank knew Karen briefly forty years ago. That hardly seems enough to get him killed now."

"Unless," Ellie said slowly, "Frank knew something about Karen's death. Something he didn't tell anyone at the time."

The sisters fell silent, contemplating this possibility. The only sound was the soft purring of Euclid, who had curled up at Angie's feet.

"But why wait forty years?" Jenna asked, breaking the silence. "If Frank knew something, why kill him now? Why didn't the criminal go after him earlier?"

Angie shook her head, frustration evident in her voice. "Maybe Frank didn't know he knew something important. Maybe it's only now, with Lorrie digging into the old case, that someone got worried."

Mr. Finch closed his book with a soft thump. "You might be onto something there, Miss Angie. Sometimes, it's not what we know that's dangerous, but what others think we know."

Before anyone could respond, the doorbell rang, its chime echoing through the house. Courtney stood, rubbing at the back of her neck. "I'll get it," she said, heading for the door with Euclid and Circe trotting at her heels.

Moments later, they heard Courtney's surprised tone, followed by hushed voices. The three sisters and Mr. Finch exchanged curious glances, their puzzle forgotten.

Courtney reappeared in the sunroom doorway, her facial expression serious. Behind her stood Lorrie Henderson, looking tense and worried, her eyes brimming with a few tears. In her trembling hand, she clutched a delicate paper flower.

Euclid let out a low hiss, while Circe stared intently at Lorrie, her tail swishing back and forth.

"I found this flower in my mailbox," Lorrie said,

her voice barely above a whisper. "What does it mean?"

Angie stood quickly, her chair scraping against the floor. "What happened?" she asked, her voice steady despite the concern evident in her eyes.

Lorrie's hand shook as she held out the paper flower. "It was in my mailbox," she repeated, her voice trembling. "I just found it."

Courtney gently suggested that Lorrie place the flower on the coffee table, careful not to touch it herself. Angie immediately reached for her phone, dialing Chief Martin's number.

While they waited for the police to arrive, Jenna poured Lorrie a glass of wine, guiding her to sit on the plush sofa. The tension in the room was heavy, broken only by the occasional nervous swish of the cats' tails.

"Lorrie," Ellie said gently, sitting beside her, "can you think of anyone who might want to frighten you? Anyone who's been acting strangely around you lately?"

Lorrie shook her head, her hands clasped tightly around the wine glass. "No, I... I've been so focused on my research. I haven't really been paying attention to... to anything else."

"What about your research?" Courtney asked

carefully. "Have you uncovered anything that might have upset someone?"

Lorrie's eyes widened slightly, a flicker of something crossing her face. "I... I'm not sure. It's all so confusing. There are so many pieces that don't seem to fit together."

Before they could probe further, the sound of car doors slamming announced the arrival of Chief Martin and another officer. The chief's face darkened with anger when he saw the paper flower on the coffee table. With a curt nod to the sisters, he instructed his officer to bag the evidence carefully and bring it to the police station.

As the officer left with the bagged flower, Chief Martin settled himself next to Lorrie on the sofa. His voice was gentle but firm as he began to question her.

"When did you find the flower?" he asked, his pen poised over his notebook.

Lorrie took a shaky breath. "About an hour ago. It was in my mailbox. As soon as I found it, I came here to show Angie."

The chief's eyes darkened. He hadn't thought Lorrie knew about the flowers left next to Frank's body. "Why does it upset you?" he probed carefully.

Lorrie's eyes widened in surprise. "Because... paper flowers were left beside Frank Sleet's body."

"How do you know this?" Chief Martin asked, his voice sharp.

"Kris Moran-Sleet told me," Lorrie admitted, brushing away a tear that had escaped down her cheek. She took a sip of wine, and as she did, the sisters could see anger beginning to replace the fear in her eyes.

Chief Martin's frown deepened. "That information wasn't supposed to be leaked to the public. I'd like you to keep this to yourself," he said, making a mental note to find out who else might know about the flowers.

Lorrie seemed to ignore the chief's statement. "Why would someone leave that flower for me?" she demanded. "Is it a threat?"

The chief tried to sound reassuring. "It may be a practical joke. People know you're looking into Karen's cold case. Someone might want to taunt you."

"Am I in danger?" Lorrie's voice rose slightly, fear creeping back in.

Chief Martin chose his words carefully. "I can't tell you for certain one way or another, but in Frank's case, the flowers were left by the body. They weren't sent prior to the attack. I'll go with you to check your house. You can show me the mailbox. I'll have an officer dust for prints, and for a few days, I'll have officers drive by your rental house. Be sure to keep your doors and windows locked and pay attention to your surroundings when you're out. Do you have pepper spray?"

"I do."

"Keep it handy, and use it if necessary. If you do use it, get away quickly. Run like heck. If anything else odd happens, call the police emergency number immediately."

As Lorrie nodded her understanding, Chief Martin stood. "Why don't we head over to your rental now? I'd like to look around."

Lorrie finished her wine and stood, thanking the sisters for their help. Angie assured her she could call anytime, while Courtney walked them to the door.

As soon as they heard the front door close, Angie turned to her sisters and Mr. Finch. "I don't like it," she said, her voice tight with worry.

"Neither do I, Miss Angie," Mr. Finch agreed, adjusting the cuff of his shirt nervously.

Euclid and Circe remained alert on the sofa,

their tails twitching back and forth as if sensing the tension in the room.

Courtney, returning from seeing their guests out, turned to Mr. Finch. "Have you been painting or drawing recently?" she asked, a hopeful note in her voice.

"I've been making art as I usually do," the older man replied knowing why Courtney asked him the question.

"Is there anything I should look at?" Angie asked.

Sometimes, when the family was working on a case, a piece of art Mr. Finch was working on included a buried clue to their current mystery that only Angie could see. Angie would sit before the artwork, go into a trance, and then she'd see a possible clue or hint about the crime.

"It wouldn't hurt," Mr. Finch said.

The sisters nodded eagerly, following Mr. Finch to his apartment off the family room. His living space was a cheerful place filled with light, and there was a sunroom dedicated to his artistic pursuits. An easel stood by the window in the sunroom, a half-finished painting resting on it.

As they gathered around the canvas, Angie felt a familiar tingling sensation. She sat in a chair and focused on the painting, a coastal scene with a lighthouse standing tall against a stormy sky. At first glance, it seemed like a typical New England seascape, but as Angie gazed at it, the image began to shift and blur.

Suddenly, she gasped, her eyes widening. "I see... I see a red notebook," she whispered. "And there's a shadow... a figure watching from the rocks."

As quickly as it had come, the vision faded. Angie blinked rapidly, coming back to herself. She turned to face her sisters and Mr. Finch, her face pale but her eyes bright with excitement.

"The red notebook," she said urgently. "Karen's notebook. I saw it in the painting."

The sisters looked at one another. Could this be the breakthrough they'd been waiting for?

"Did you see where it was?" Ellie asked eagerly.

Angie shook her head, frustration evident in her voice. "No, just that it exists. It's still out there somewhere. It hasn't been destroyed."

Jenna placed a comforting hand on Angie's arm. "Now we know that the notebook is still around. It's a real lead."

As they made their way back to the family room, the mystery surrounding Karen LeBlanc and Frank Sleet was front and center in their minds. The paper flower left for Lorrie, the red notebook, the shadowy figure - all small details that might eventually reveal some answers.

"We need to be careful," Courtney said as they settled back around the puzzle table. "If someone's willing to threaten Lorrie, they might come after us, too."

Ellie said, "We should stay together as much as possible. Try not to go anywhere alone, especially at night."

"And we need to keep a closer eye on Lorrie," Angie added. "Whether she knows it or not, she's in the middle of all this."

Mr. Finch, who had followed them back to the family room, spoke up. "Perhaps it's time to talk more to Ms. Henderson. She might have information that could help, even if she doesn't realize it."

The sisters had been cautious about fully trusting Lorrie, but Mr. Finch had a point.

Angie yawned and sipped from her water glass. She often felt exhausted after experiencing a vision. "That might be a good idea. For now, let's focus on what we know. The notebook exists, and maybe someone is worried enough about it to start making threats."

As night fell over Sweet Cove, the puzzle on the table lay ignored for now, a fitting metaphor for the larger mystery they were trying to solve. Unlike the jigsaw pieces scattered before them, the pieces of the real-life puzzle were not all in plain sight.

The case seemed to be taking a dark turn, and in Sweet Cove, as in life, the darkest hour often came just before the dawn.

16

The morning sun streamed through the large windows of the Victorian mansion's kitchen, shining over the bustling scene inside. The air was filled with the rich aroma of freshly brewed coffee and the sweet scent of cake batter.

Perched on top of the refrigerator, Euclid and Circe surveyed the kitchen with regal indifference, their tails swishing lazily as they watched the morning routine going on below them.

Ellie moved around the kitchen, preparing breakfast for the B&B guests. Her hands deftly arranged hard-boiled eggs on a serving dish, which she placed on a pantry cart alongside platters of crispy bacon, plump sausages, a colorful bowl of fruit salad, and a plate of golden, flaky croissants still warm from the oven.

At the kitchen table, Courtney and Mr. Finch sat engrossed in their morning newspapers, occasionally taking bites of their fried eggs and toast. The gentle rustle of paper mingled with the soft clink of cutlery against plates.

Angie stood at the kitchen island, her hands covered in flour as she mixed cake batter in a large bowl. She paused occasionally to take a sip from her coffee mug, her eyes distant as she mulled over the events of the previous night.

The side door swung open, and Jenna entered with her daughter Libby in tow. "Morning, everyone."

The little girl's eyes lit up at the sight of her aunts, who gave the little girl hugs and kisses.

Angie said, "Gigi's in the family room."

With a quick hug to her mother's legs, Libby dashed off to play with her cousin.

Jenna poured herself a cup of coffee and settled onto a stool at the kitchen island to watch Angie bake.

"Have you heard anything from the organizer of the Academy Awards show about your jewelry being included in the gift baskets?" Angie asked.

Jenna shook her head. "It's too early yet. I just shipped them some samples of my work about five days ago. I think it will take months to hear back."

"We'll keep our fingers crossed," Angie told her twin with a supportive smile.

Suddenly, Courtney perked up, her eyes widening as she read something on her phone. "Listen to this," she said, her voice filled with excitement. "There's a paper flower craft workshop tonight at the Lilac Hill Farm. I think we should go." She looked up at her sisters, her blue eyes sparkling with enthusiasm. "Who wants to come?"

"A paper flower craft workshop?" Ellie echoed, pausing in her breakfast preparations.

"They're going to teach how to make paper flowers," Courtney explained. "It might be good to go. We could meet the instructors and the participants. We could ask questions about people who might have taken the class recently. Maybe our killer took one of their classes."

Angie added eggs to the cake batter. "That's actually a good idea. I'll go with you. If we don't get any leads, we'll at least learn a new craft."

Jenna shook her head, a wry smile on her face. "Could you even make one of those flowers without thinking of Frank Sleet's murder?"

"Some time would have to pass, I guess," Ellie suggested, wiping her hands on her apron. "I'll go, too."

Jenna's smile widened. "I'm not going to be left out. I'll go along as well." She turned to Mr. Finch, who was listening to the conversation with interest. "What about you, Mr. Finch? Want to join us?"

The older gentleman chuckled, his eyes twinkling. "I believe I'll leave the craftwork to all of you," he told her with a fond smile.

Courtney was already tapping at her phone screen. "I'll sign us all up," she said decisively.

The kitchen buzzed as the sisters continued to discuss the upcoming workshop. The paper flower class could be just the lead they needed to help with the case.

As they finalized their plans for the evening, the familiar routines of the morning continued. Angie poured her cake batter into a pan and slid it into the oven, filling the kitchen with the promise of a sweet treat to come. Ellie wheeled her cart of breakfast items toward the dining room, ready to greet the B&B guests.

Courtney finished her breakfast and stood, stretching. "I should head to the candy shop," she said, glancing at the clock. "I'll see you all this evening for the workshop."

As the sisters began to disperse to their various responsibilities, there was a palpable sense of anticipation in the air. The paper flower workshop might seem like an innocent craft class to most, but for the Roseland sisters, it represented a potential breakthrough in their investigation.

Angie watched as her sisters filed out of the kitchen, each lost in their own thoughts about the evening ahead. She turned back to her baking, her mind already planning some questions they could ask at the workshop. Who had attended recent classes? Had anyone shown an unusual interest in the craft? Could the instructors remember any students who stood out?

The oven timer chimed, and as she pulled out the golden, fragrant cake, she couldn't help but feel a glimmer of hope. Perhaps this seemingly simple craft class would help in unraveling the web of mystery surrounding Frank Sleet's murder and its possible connection to Karen LeBlanc's decades-old cold case.

Tonight, they'd take another step in their investigation, armed with curiosity, determination, and the willingness to follow even the most delicate of paper trails.

The early evening sun was low in the sky, shining a soft light over the rolling countryside as Ellie maneuvered the van along the winding road toward Lilac Hill Farm. The sisters chatted excitedly, their anticipation growing as they neared their destination. After a short fifteen-minute drive, Ellie turned onto a dirt driveway, the van kicking up a small cloud of dust as they passed lush green fields and towering shade trees.

As they pulled into the gravel parking lot, the sisters caught sight of the farm's huge red barn, its weathered wood glowing warmly in the fading sunlight. Smaller outbuildings dotted the property, including a quaint store where the farm sold its bounty of fresh produce, honey, eggs, jewelry, and an array of handcrafted items.

"Look!" Jenna pointed as they walked toward the main barn. "The corn maze is almost ready. Remember when we used to come here as kids?"

Angie smiled, memories flooding back. "And

now they've got so much more - music events, pizza nights, even a petting zoo. It's become a really great attraction."

Courtney said enthusiastically, "Don't forget the apple picking and homemade ice cream. This place is magical during the holidays."

As they entered the spacious barn, the sisters were greeted by the sight of neatly arranged tables and chairs, each place set with an array of colorful papers, scissors, and other crafting supplies. At the front of the room stood a large whiteboard, ready for the instructors to demonstrate the steps in the intricate art of paper flower making.

More participants filtered in, filling the barn with a buzz of excited chatter. Soon, twenty women had gathered, some returning students eager to tackle more challenging designs and others who were complete novices to the craft.

The refreshment table near the back of the barn quickly became busy. The rich aroma of freshly brewed coffee and the sweet scent of apple muffins from the farm store created an inviting atmosphere that encouraged conversation.

Angie and her sisters circulated, their ears pricked for any useful information as they sipped their drinks and nibbled on muffins. They overheard snippets of conversation about previous classes, the intricacy of certain designs, and the sense of pride in creating something beautiful.

As the clock struck seven, two women made their way to the front of the room. The taller of the two, with auburn hair pulled back in an upsweep, introduced herself as Paige. Her colleague, a petite blonde with a warm smile, was Emily.

Paige began with a brief history of paper flowers, her voice carrying easily through the barn. "Paper flowers have been crafted for centuries," she explained, "with early examples found in ancient Egypt and China. The art form gained popularity in Victorian England as a way to bring beauty into the home year-round."

Emily then took over, discussing various techniques. "There are many ways to create paper flowers," she said, gesturing to a display of intricate blooms. "From simple origami folds to complex crepe paper sculptures, each method produces unique and beautiful results."

The instructors then launched into a step-by-step demonstration, their hands moving with practiced ease as they crafted a delicate rose. They explained each fold and cut, their instructions clear and patient.

"Start with a square of paper," Paige instructed, holding up a vibrant red sheet. "Fold it diagonally, then unfold and fold it diagonally in the other direction. These creases will guide your petals."

Emily continued, "Now, fold each corner into the center, creating a smaller square. This forms the base of your flower."

The sisters, along with the rest of the class, followed along, studies in concentration as they mimicked the instructors' movements.

"For the petals," Paige demonstrated, "gently curl the edges of each folded triangle outward. This gives your flower dimension and a more realistic appearance."

As the class progressed, the barn filled with the soft rustle of paper and occasional murmurs of frustration or delight. The Roseland sisters found themselves caught up in the process, their concerns about the case momentarily forgotten as they focused on crafting their delicate blooms.

By the end of the two-hour session, twenty unique paper flowers adorned the tables, each an example of its creator's patience and newly discovered skills.

Angie held up her pale pink rose, a smile of satisfaction on her face. "It's not half bad."

Ellie laughed, comparing her deep red bloom to Angie's. "Who knew we had such hidden talents?"

As the class began to disperse, the sisters lingered, helping to tidy up while engaging the instructors and other participants in conversation. They asked casual questions about previous classes, trying to gauge if anyone suspicious had attended recent sessions.

"Have you had any particularly memorable students lately?" Courtney asked Paige as they gathered leftover supplies.

Paige thought for a moment. "We've had quite a diverse group over the past few months. There was a gentleman a few weeks back who seemed very intent on perfecting his technique. He said he was making decorations for his daughter's wedding."

The sisters shared quick glances with each other, but nothing about the man's story seemed overtly suspicious.

As they made their way back to the van, they compared notes on what they'd learned - or rather, hadn't learned.

"Well," Angie said as they pulled out of the parking lot, "I didn't pick up on anything unusual.

Though I did have a moment of anxiety when choosing my paper color."

Courtney couldn't resist teasing her sister. "Oh no, the great Angie Roseland, felled by the mighty decision of pink versus red."

The others laughed.

"Well, anyway," Ellie said as she maneuvered the van along the winding country road, the headlights cutting through the gathering darkness, "the evening wasn't a total waste. At least we learned a new craft tonight."

"So says the pessimistic optimist," Courtney joked, earning another round of laughter from her sisters.

As they drove home, the conversation turned more serious. "Do you think we're barking up the wrong tree?" Jenna asked, voicing the concern they'd all been considering.

Angie shook her head. "I don't know. It seemed like a solid lead, but maybe we're grasping at straws."

"Or paper flowers," Courtney quipped, unable to resist.

Ellie, ever the voice of reason, spoke up. "Let's not discount it entirely. Even if we didn't find a direct link tonight, we've learned more about the craft. That knowledge might come in handy later."

The paper flowers the sisters had created sat carefully on their laps, delicate reminders of the evening's activities and the mystery they were trying to unravel.

As they neared Sweet Cove, the familiar sights of their hometown coming into view, Angie suddenly sat up straighter. "Wait a minute," she said, her voice filled with excitement. "What if we're looking at this all wrong?"

Her sisters turned to her.

"What do you mean?" Jenna asked.

"We've been assuming that the killer learned to make paper flowers recently, maybe even in a class like this," Angie explained, her words coming faster as her idea took shape. "But what if they've known how to make them for years? What if it's a skill they've had since... since Karen's time?"

A heavy silence fell over the van as Angie's words sank in. Could the paper flowers be a link not just to Frank's murder, but to Karen's as well?

"We need to look into any paper flower enthusiasts or clubs that were around forty years ago," Courtney said, her instincts kicking in.

Ellie's hands tightened on the steering wheel. "And we need to find out if there were any paper flowers associated with Karen's case that weren't made public."

The evening might not have provided the breakthrough they'd hoped for, but it had sparked something new to look into. The delicate paper blooms they carried inside were no longer just crafts, but maybe a key to unlocking two mysteries.

17

It was late afternoon, and Angie was just pulling a tray of golden, flaky croissants from the oven when she looked up to see Chief Martin stepping into the bake shop, an expression of weariness on his face that had become all too familiar lately.

"Afternoon, Chief," Angie greeted warmly, setting the tray on the counter. "Coffee?"

Chief Martin settled onto a stool at the counter. "Please. Black as night and strong enough to wake the dead."

Angie chuckled as she poured him a steaming mug. "Rough day?"

The chief took a long sip before answering. "Just a lot on my mind. This case ... it's like trying to put together a picture where half the pieces are missing and the other half don't seem to fit."

Angie nodded sympathetically, her own thoughts turning to the paper flower class from the previous evening.

"Chief," she said, her voice dropping slightly, "I have to ask again. Have you been able to find any evidence of paper flowers associated with Karen LeBlanc's murder?"

Chief Martin's forehead scrunched up as he set down his mug. "I've been looking into that. There's no mention of paper flowers at the crime scene when Karen was killed. Of course, it was forty years ago and some of the information is lost."

Angie leaned against the counter, her blue eyes bright. "We all went to a craft session last night to learn how to make paper flowers. We talked to the instructors and the other participants, trying to see if anyone who'd attended previous sessions had seemed ... off somehow."

The chief raised an eyebrow. "And?"

Angie sighed, a hint of disappointment in her voice. "Nothing out of the ordinary. But it got us thinking - what if the killer has known how to make these flowers for years? Maybe even since Karen's time?"

Chief Martin's expression was thoughtful. "It's an interesting theory. We shouldn't discount it, but there's no indication of paper flowers at Karen's murder." He paused, seeming to consider something. "Actually, Angie, there's something I wanted to ask you. I've talked to an old friend of Karen's, but I think you might get something more from the woman. I was wondering if you and one of your sisters might be willing to interview her. Sometimes a different approach can uncover new information."

Angie's eyes lit up. "Of course. We'd be happy to help. Who is she?"

"Her name is Carolyn Thorn," the chief replied. "She and Karen were close friends back in the day. They met in college. Carolyn and her husband live about thirty minutes from town."

As Chief Martin provided more details about Carolyn and what he'd learned so far, Angie listened closely.

"I'll talk to my sisters and set something up," Angie said. "Is there anything specific you want us to focus on?"

The chief thought for a moment. "Just keep an open mind. Carolyn's shared the basics with me, but I wondered if there was more to the story. Maybe you'll pick up on something I missed."

Angie nodded, understanding the unspoken trust in the chief's request. He hoped the sisters' unique abilities might uncover some clues or details.

As they continued to chat, the bakery began to fill with the mid-afternoon rush of customers. Angie moved efficiently behind the counter, serving fresh pastries and steaming cups of coffee, but her mind was already on the upcoming interview with Carolyn Thorn.

When there was a lull in customers, Angie turned back to Chief Martin. "Chief, about those paper flowers ... do you think it's possible they're some kind of signature? Have there been any other crimes where paper flowers were left behind?"

The chief's expression turned grave. "It's possible that we might be dealing with someone who's been active for a lot longer than we initially thought. There are no other incidents that we know of where paper flowers were left. The other thing to remember is the killer may have made reference to Karen LeBlanc's murder just to throw us off the track."

The idea hung in the air between them. If there was no connection at all between Frank and Karen's murders, they may have been wasting a lot of time.

As Chief Martin prepared to leave, he paused before heading to the door. "Angie, be careful with this interview. If Carolyn knows something she hasn't shared yet, there might be a reason for her silence."

Angie nodded, understanding the warning. "We'll be careful. We'll let you know what we find out."

After the chief left, Angie busied herself with the morning rush, but her mind was far from the tasks at hand. The possibility of interviewing Karen's old friend, the mystery of the paper flowers, the potential for a breakthrough in the case - it all swirled in her head, like the steam rising from the coffee pots.

During a quiet moment, she slipped into the back room to call her sisters. They quickly agreed that Angie and Courtney would handle the interview with Carolyn Thorn.

She returned to the front of the bakery, greeting customers with a warm smile that hid her confused thoughts. Sweet Cove bustled around her, its residents going about their day unaware of the mysteries slowly unraveling in their midst.

As the day wore on, Angie was anxious to close up shop and begin preparing for the interview. She and Courtney had agreed to visit Carolyn Thorn the following afternoon, giving them time to research and prepare their questions.

She really hoped something would come of it.

The quaint café two towns over from Sweet Cove bustled with the late morning crowd as Angie and Courtney pushed open the door. Angie's eyes scanned the room, quickly spotting who they were meeting - a slim, athletic woman with a chin-length brown bob, seated at a corner table. As they approached, the woman looked up, her brown eyes warm with recognition.

"Carolyn?" Angie asked, extending her hand. "I'm Angie Roseland, and this is my sister Courtney. Thank you so much for meeting with us."

Carolyn stood, shaking their hands with a firm grip. "Of course. I have to admit, I was intrigued by your call. It's been years since anyone's asked about Karen. I spoke with Chief Martin from Sweet Cove. It seems the cold case might be reopened?"

"The police are taking a new look at the case," Courtney explained.

As they settled into their seats, a waiter appeared to take their orders. Once he had bustled away, Angie smiled at Carolyn.

"We really appreciate you taking the time to talk with us," she said. "We're hoping you might be able to shed some light on Karen's time in Sweet Cove."

Carolyn nodded, a wistful smile touching her lips. "It's strange to think back on those days. Mike and I have been so busy with our realty business and our grandkids, it feels like another lifetime."

"You've known your husband since kindergarten, right?" Courtney asked, her investigative instincts kicking in.

Carolyn's smile widened. "That's right. We were high school sweethearts and married right after college. Four kids and eight grandkids later, here we are."

The waiter returned with their drinks, momentarily interrupting the conversation. Once he had left, Angie gently steered the conversation back to Karen.

"You mentioned to Chief Martin that you knew Karen at college?"

Carolyn wrapped her hands around her steaming mug. "We met in a business class and became friends. We lost touch for a while after graduation, but then I ran into her again when we were in our late twenties. We were both busy with careers, and I had two little kids already. It was hard to keep in touch. She was in the area doing a story on the best New England places to visit in the summer, and we reconnected."

"Did you spend much time together during her visit?" Courtney asked.

"We got together quite a few times for dinner or a walk. It was nice to catch up." Carolyn's expression darkened. "I was horrified when I found out she'd been murdered."

Angie said, "I'm so sorry. It must have been a terrible shock."

Carolyn looked down, taking a moment to compose herself before continuing.

"Did Karen seem like herself when you met up with her?" Angie asked gently.

Carolyn considered the question. "For the most part, but sometimes she seemed stressed. She had deadlines to meet every week. Every Sunday, the news outlet highlighted one place in New England. They did that every Sunday from May to mid-August. Karen was using Sweet Cove as her base to write about places in Massachusetts, New Hampshire, and Maine. She'd already been in Rhode Island and Connecticut."

Courtney asked, "Was she worried about anyone or anything besides her deadlines?"

A flicker of something crossed Carolyn's face. "She'd been arguing a lot with her boyfriend Winthrop Kelly. He wanted more from her than she was willing to give. He was interested in marriage, and Karen, at least at that point, wanted to remain independent."

Carolyn paused to take a sip of her coffee before continuing. "While she was in Sweet Cove, there was also a man who wanted to date her, but she didn't want to complicate things so she'd told him no. He kept after her and she said it stressed her out. She wanted to focus on her stories."

"Did she tell you his name?" Angie asked, trying to keep her voice casual.

Carolyn shook her head. "If she did, I don't recall what it was."

Angie took a deep breath, considering her next question carefully. "Do you think Karen was working on something besides the travel pieces? Did she ever allude to working on something that might be dangerous?"

Carolyn blinked as a look of surprise washed over her face. "Dangerous? Like what?"

"We don't know," Courtney interjected smoothly. "We were wondering if she was investigating a more serious story."

Carolyn's brow furrowed in thought. "I don't think so. She had lots of ideas, but I don't think she was actively working on anything else. She was probably doing research on a number of story ideas she had, but the summer fun places articles seemed to be all she had time for."

As the conversation wound down, Angie and Courtney thanked Carolyn for her time and insights. They exchanged pleasantries with promises to keep in touch before the sisters made their way back to the parking lot.

Once they were safely in their car, Angie turned to Courtney, her eyes wide. "Carolyn said someone was pressuring Karen to date him. Could that have been Frank Sleet?"

Courtney looked thoughtful. "I wondered the very same thing. Did Frank get angry when Karen wouldn't date him?"

"Angry enough to kill her?" Angie mused, her voice barely above a whisper.

Courtney's brow furrowed. "But then who killed Frank?"

Angie ran a hand over her face. "Maybe the two crimes have nothing to do with one another," she thought out loud. "Maybe there are actually two killers, and we've been wrong all this time thinking the same person killed Frank and Karen."

She started the engine with a long sigh.

18

The warm light of the family room lamps created a snug atmosphere for the gathered Roseland clan. Outside, the autumn breeze whispered through the trees, occasionally rattling the windows, as if trying to join the family movie night. The scent of freshly popped popcorn mingled with the faint aroma of pumpkin spice candles, creating a perfect setting for a quiet evening in.

Josh and Angie settled onto the plush sofa, their fingers intertwined. Beside them, Jenna and Tom cuddled close, while Jack and Ellie sat together in the oversized armchair. Rufus and Courtney sprawled on the thick area rug, propped up on a mountain of pillows. Mr. Finch sat in his favorite easy chair, a twinkle in his eye as he watched the family he'd come to love as his own.

Euclid and Circe, the family's feline companions, prowled the perimeter of the room, their tails swishing as they made their rounds.

Chatting away, the group was enjoying drinks and snacks before the opening credits of the crime movie would play across the TV screen.

Mr. Finch was passing around bowls of popcorn when he approached Angie. "Are you sensing something?"

Angie's eyes widened and she whispered, "I have been for hours. Something's wrong, but I don't know what it is." She hadn't been able to shake the feeling of unease that had been plaguing her all day. She shifted in her seat, trying to get comfortable, but the nagging sensation persisted.

"I agree," Mr. Finch murmured, settling beside her while the other family members chatted and laughed, oblivious to the undercurrent of tension.

As if drawn by an invisible force, Euclid and Circe padded over, settling at Angie and Mr. Finch's feet. Their tails flicked back and forth, a clear sign of their agitation.

"Euclid and Circe can feel it, too," Mr. Finch observed, running a soothing hand over their fur.

Angie rubbed her arms as a shiver ran through her despite the room's warmth. "My skin feels like it's getting jolted by an electrical current," she confessed. "What's going on?"

Mr. Finch closed his eyes, his facial muscles tightening in concentration. When he opened them again, he turned to face Angie, his expression grave. "Have you talked with Lorrie recently?"

The color drained from Angie's face. "Come to think of it, I haven't seen her for two days. She hasn't come into the bake shop," she said, standing abruptly. "Come on."

Without a word to the others, Angie and Mr. Finch slipped out of the family room, their departure going unnoticed amidst the laughter and chatter.

In the kitchen, Angie's trembling fingers fumbled with her phone as she dialed Lorrie's number. The call went straight to voicemail, Lorrie's cheerful greeting worsening the growing knot of dread in Angie's stomach.

"I'm worried," she said, her voice barely above a whisper.

Mr. Finch's eyes held a glimmer of determination. "Let's take a little ride to her rental house," he suggested.

Angie grabbed her keys from the pegboard near the back door. "I'll text Jenna and let her know we'll be right back," she said, her fingers flying over the phone's keyboard.

The cool night air hit them as they stepped outside, carrying with it the scent of fallen leaves and distant woodsmoke. Angie's car stood waiting in the driveway, its metal gleaming dully in the moonlight.

As they climbed in, her hands gripped the steering wheel, her knuckles white. The short drive to Lorrie's rental seemed to stretch on for hours, with each turn of the winding road ratcheting up their anxiety.

Finally, Angie pulled into the driveway of a small cottage, its windows dark and uninviting. Lorrie's car sat in front of them.

"Her car's here," Angie said, her voice tight.

They exited the car, the crunch of gravel under their feet seeming unnaturally loud in the quiet night. As they approached the front door, the porch light flickered on, triggered by their movement. The sudden illumination cast long shadows across the neatly trimmed lawn, creating an eerie play of light and dark.

Mr. Finch reached out and rang the doorbell. Its

cheerful chime echoed through the house, but no answering footsteps came. They waited, the seconds ticking by with agonizing slowness.

"I'm going to call her phone again," Angie said, her voice trembling slightly. Once more, the call went to voicemail. "I'm worried," she repeated, her eyes wide with fear.

Unable to contain her anxiety any longer, Angie began pounding on the front door, her fists making a dull thud against the solid wood. "Lorrie!" she called out, her voice cracking. "Lorrie, are you there?"

Mr. Finch placed a calming hand on her shoulder. "Let's go around back," he suggested, his voice low and steady.

They made their way around the side of the house, the beam of Mr. Finch's phone flashlight cutting through the darkness. The backyard was small but well-maintained, with a patio set that looked like it had rarely been used.

At the back door, they rang the bell again, the sound seeming to mock them with its cheerful tone. Still, no response came from within the house.

Mr. Finch's face was grim as he pulled out his phone. "I'm going to call Chief Martin," he said, his fingers already dialing the number.

While Mr. Finch spoke in hushed tones to the

police chief, Angie moved to one of the windows. Standing on her tiptoes, she peered inside, her hands cupped around her eyes to block out the glare of the porch light.

For a moment, all she could see was darkness. Then, as her eyes adjusted, details began to emerge. A coffee table with scattered papers. An open laptop. And there, just visible beyond the edge of the sofa...

For a moment, Angie's heart seemed to stop, then started again with a painful thud. "Mr. Finch," she gasped, her voice barely audible. "Mr. Finch!"

He was at her side in an instant. "What is it?" he asked, his voice tight with concern.

Angie's words came out in a horrified whisper. "Lorrie's on the floor. She's bleeding. I think she might be dead."

The world seemed to tilt on its axis as her words sank in. Mr. Finch's face paled, but his voice remained steady as he spoke into the phone. "Chief, we need you at Lorrie Henderson's rental. Now. It's an emergency."

As they waited for the police to arrive, Angie and Mr. Finch stood frozen, their eyes fixed on the dark window that had revealed such a terrible sight. The night seemed to press in on them, full of unseen dangers and unspoken fears.

"This was the reason I often felt anxious and uneasy when Lorrie was around," Angie said. "It was because she was in danger. She wasn't untrustworthy, and she wasn't working against us. I should have figured that out." A tear slipped from the young woman's eye.

Mr. Finch wrapped her in a hug. "It's very difficult to make sense of our feelings and premonitions. Sometimes, what we feel just isn't clear at all."

In the distance, the faint wail of sirens began to grow louder, heralding the approach of help, but for Angie and Mr. Finch, standing in the shadows of Lorrie's darkened home, the sirens carried an ominous question: had Frank's killer struck again?

The peaceful night now stood shattered, replaced by a darkness that seemed to seep into their hearts. As blue and red lights began to flash in the distance, Angie and Mr. Finch wore expressions of worry and sadness.

The sirens grew louder, piercing the quiet night, and Angie's heart raced. Who had done this? Why Lorrie? And most chillingly, were they still out there, watching from the shadows?

As Chief Martin's car screeched to a halt in front of the house, followed closely by an ambulance and more police vehicles, Angie and Mr.

Finch braced themselves for what was to come. The night was far from over, and the darkness that had fallen over Sweet Cove seemed deeper than before.

The night air had grown cooler, or maybe it was just the chill of fear that made Angie and Mr. Finch shiver as they waited outside Lorrie's rental house. The once-quiet street now buzzed with activity, the flashing lights of police cars and an ambulance painting the neighborhood in an eerie red and blue glow.

The sound of tires on gravel announced the arrival of Angie's sisters. They spilled out of Ellie's van, their faces etched with worry and confusion.

"What's happened?" Courtney questioned, her voice tight with concern. "Why did you come here?"

Angie spoke softly, "We ... we had a feeling. Something felt wrong. I've felt it all day."

Mr. Finch's normally jovial face was serious. "We both felt a sense of anxiety, a foreboding, if you will. We decided to check on Lorrie, given recent events."

The sisters listened in stunned silence as Angie and Mr. Finch recounted their evening, from the nagging feeling of unease to the horrifying discovery at the window.

Before they could ask any more questions, the back door of the house opened. Chief Martin emerged, his face a mask of professional detachment, but his eyes betrayed the gravity of the situation. He walked over to the family, his steps heavy with the news he carried.

"I'm sorry to tell you," he began, his voice low and somber, "Lorrie Henderson was murdered. A single bullet to the chest. A paper flower was found next to her body."

A collective gasp went up from the group. Angie felt her knees go weak, and Jenna reached out to steady her.

"The flower, however, did not contain a message," the chief continued, his voice taking on a more official tone. "We'll be confiscating Lorrie's notes and her laptop. They might provide some leads."

He paused, his eyes scanning the faces of the Roseland sisters and Mr. Finch. "I know this is a lot to ask, but ... would you come in and look around? Her body is still on the floor. It's covered with a sheet. I understand if you can't do it."

Ellie's face paled, horror evident in her wide

eyes, but after a moment, she nodded. "We'll do it," she whispered.

As they entered the house, the atmosphere changed. The interior that had once been Lorrie's temporary home now felt cold and alien. The smell of gunpowder lingered in the air, mingling with a coppery scent that made Angie's stomach churn.

They moved slowly into the living room where Lorrie's body lay partially obscured by the coffee table and a sheet. The sisters and Mr. Finch spread out, each drawn to different areas of the room.

Jenna suddenly stiffened, her gaze fixed on a corner of the room. "Karen," she whispered, her voice trembling. But as quickly as it had appeared, the ghostly spirit of Karen LeBlanc vanished, leaving Jenna shaken and confused.

Angie, Ellie, and Courtney wandered the room, their faces hard with a mix of emotions. Each sister felt waves of conflicting sensations washing over them - hate, jealousy, and rage seemed to permeate the very air around them.

Mr. Finch, meanwhile, had bent down to pick up one of Lorrie's shoes that had fallen near the body. He held it gently in his hands for a few moments, his eyes closed in concentration. When he opened them, his face was ashen.

Chief Martin walked over to him. "Mr. Finch?"

"The killer was familiar to Lorrie," he said, his voice barely above a whisper. "The killer is someone from town."

Angie's heart nearly stopped at these words. The idea that the killer was someone they might know, someone who walked the streets of Sweet Cove alongside them, was almost too terrible to consider.

Chief Martin took a deep breath. "Are you sure about that, Mr. Finch?"

Mr. Finch said, "As sure as I can be, Chief. The impression was quite strong."

The chief's face hardened. "That certainly narrows down our suspect pool, but it also means we need to be extra cautious. No one is above suspicion at this point."

As the reality of the situation sank in, a heavy silence fell over the room. The sisters huddled together, seeking comfort in each other's presence. Mr. Finch stood slightly apart, his eyes distant, as if still processing what he had sensed.

Who in Sweet Cove could have done this? Who had the motive, the opportunity? And most chillingly, who might be next?

"Chief," Angie said, breaking the silence, "what

about the paper flower? Was it... was it like the ones left with Frank Sleet?"

Chief Martin said, "Identical, as far as we can tell, which means we're dealing with the same killer, or at least someone who knows about the previous murders."

Courtney asked, "Was anything taken? Any sign of what the killer might have been looking for?"

"It's hard to say at this point," the chief replied. "We'll need to go through everything carefully, but at first glance, it doesn't appear to be a robbery gone wrong. This was targeted."

As they continued to discuss the scene, Angie's eyes swept the room, taking in the scattered papers, the open laptop, and the half-empty coffee mug on the side table. What had Lorrie discovered that had cost her life?

"We should go," Ellie said softly, her face pale. "Let the police do their job."

While the others filed out of the house, Angie cast one last look at the scene. Lorrie's body was a stark reminder of the danger they might all be in.

Outside, the night seemed darker than before, the shadows deeper and more menacing. The sisters huddled close, drawing strength from each other's presence.

"What do we do now?" Jenna asked, her voice trembling slightly.

Angie stood straighter. "We do what we always do. We keep digging, and we don't stop until we uncover who's behind this."

The others nodded in agreement. As they prepared to leave, Chief Martin approached one last time.

"I don't need to tell you to be careful," he said, his voice low and serious. "Whoever did this is still out there, and they're not afraid to kill to keep their secrets."

With those chilling words hanging in the air, the Roseland sisters and Mr. Finch made their way back to their vehicles.

As they pulled up to the Victorian, its warm lights like a beacon in the darkness, their beloved hometown now felt like a place of secrets and hidden dangers.

They climbed the porch steps and entered the house, and the door closed behind them, shutting out the night and its terrors.

19

Angie and Ellie were in a somber mood as they made their way up the winding walkway through the perfectly manicured lawn to the front door of Kris Moran-Slate's home. They could smell the faint aroma of paint coming through the open windows, hinting at the renovations taking place inside. Chief Martin requested they interview Kris again, in light of Lorrie's murder.

Angie knocked softly, her knuckles barely grazing the polished wood of the door. The sound seemed to echo in the quiet neighborhood.

After a moment, the door creaked open. Kris Moran-Sleet's once-vibrant appearance had faded after the murder of her husband, replaced by a woman who seemed to carry the weight of the world on her shoulders. Dark circles shadowed her eyes, and her clothes hung loosely on her frame, as if she had lost weight rapidly. Her hair, once neatly styled, now hung limp around her face, adding to her overall appearance of exhaustion and grief.

"Angie, Ellie," she greeted them, her voice just a whisper, "please, come in."

As they stepped into the foyer, Angie noticed the oppressive atmosphere that seemed to permeate the house. It was as if a dark cloud had settled over the once-cheerful home, dimming the light and muffling the sounds. The air inside felt heavy and stagnant, as if grief itself had moved into the place.

Kris led them to the living room, gesturing for them to take a seat on the plush sofa. The sisters sank onto the soft cushions, noting the layer of dust that had settled on the nearby coffee table. It was clear that housekeeping had fallen by the wayside in the wake of tragedy. Kris settled into an armchair across from them, her movements slow and deliberate, as if every action required great effort.

"Thank you for seeing us," Angie began gently. "We know this must be very difficult for you."

Kris's gaze fixed on a point somewhere beyond the sisters. Her eyes seemed to focus on a framed photograph on the mantel showing her and Frank in happier times. The contrast between the smiling couple in the picture and the sad, empty woman before them was heartbreaking.

"The kitchen is being renovated," she said abruptly, her voice tinged with pain. "I just can't go into that room for any length of time. I try to avoid it. It's where ... where Frank..." She trailed off, swallowing hard before continuing. "Frank died in that room. I just can't stay in the house with all that bad energy seeping from the kitchen."

Ellie looked at the woman with compassion. "Have you listed the house already?"

Kris shook her head, a strand of hair falling across her face. She brushed it away impatiently. "Not yet, but I've retained a real estate agent. Betty Hayes. Do you know her?"

"Yes, we do," Angie replied with a bit of a smile. "She's a good friend of ours. You can't go wrong having Betty as your agent."

A flicker of relief passed over Kris's face, momentarily lightening her features. "That's good to know. She came highly recommended to me."

There was a moment of silence, broken only by the sound of construction from the kitchen. The rhythmic pounding of hammers seemed to underscore the tension in the room. Angie took a deep breath, preparing herself for the more difficult questions they needed to ask.

"Kris," she began carefully, "have you had any thoughts about who could have attacked your husband?"

The change in Kris's demeanor was immediate. Her face fell, the lines of grief etching themselves deeper into her features. She clasped her hands tightly in her lap, her knuckles turning white with the force of her grip.

"No, I haven't," she said, in a whispery tone. "I have no idea who could have done this. Frank was well-liked. His students enjoyed his classes. His colleagues had nothing but good things to say about him." Her voice grew stronger, tinged with a hint of desperation. "I know the police don't think it was a random attack, but I have to disagree. I can't think of one person who would want to hurt Frank."

Ellie tried to process Kris's words and body language. She noticed a slight tremor in the woman's hands, a detail that seemed at odds with her strong denial that Frank had known his killer.

"Have there been any more calls from Frank's colleague who was phoning him in the evenings?" Ellie asked, her tone gentle but probing.

Kris shook her head, frustration creeping into

her voice. "I wouldn't know. The police confiscated his phone. Anyway, the police discovered it was a colleague who heard Frank was moving here to the area. He was trying to talk Frank into accepting a lecturer position at the nearby university." She sighed heavily, rubbing the back of her neck. "I didn't want Frank to work. I wanted him to enjoy his retirement, take up a new hobby, golf, hike, and spend some time at the beach. But knowing Frank, I bet he was going to accept that job." Her voice broke slightly as she added, "It doesn't matter now, does it? My life has really fallen apart."

Angie's heart ached for the woman, but she knew they needed to press on. "Kris, I know this is painful, but can you run us through what happened that day? Every detail, no matter how small, could be important."

A flash of annoyance crossed Kris's face, quickly replaced by a look of resignation. "I've gone through it many times already," she said, her tone weary.

"I know," Angie said soothingly, "but it helps to describe what happened several times. It's very possible the brain will come up with some new details. It can be very helpful to the case."

Kris leaned back on the chair, letting out a long sigh. Her gaze drifted to the window where the late afternoon sunlight was creating dappled shadows through the leaves of a nearby tree. When she spoke, her voice sounded robotic, as if she were reciting a well-rehearsed script.

"I went to the grocery store. Frank stayed here to do some things around the house. Later in the day, we planned to head to the beach. I got home with the groceries and went inside. I called his name. There was no answer." Her voice faltered for a moment, and she closed her eyes briefly before continuing. "I went into the kitchen and saw him there on the floor." She paused, swallowing hard before continuing. "There was so much blood. I knew he was dead. I was afraid whoever killed him was still in the house, so I ran outside and called the police. You know the rest."

The sisters noted the detached way Kris reported the events. There was something off about her tone, a disconnect between the awful scene she described and the almost clinical way she narrated it.

Ellie decided to change tack, hoping a different line of questioning might yield more insights. "Did you become friendly with Lorrie Henderson recently?" she asked, her tone deliberately casual.

Confusion flickered across Kris's face, her brow furrowing. "Who?"

"She's the true crime writer who was in Sweet Cove for a couple of months researching a cold case," Ellie explained, watching Kris's reaction closely.

Recognition dawned on Kris's face, but there was something else there, too. It was gone so quickly that Ellie couldn't be sure what it was.

"Oh, yes, sorry," Kris said, her voice suddenly tighter. "I heard she was killed. Do the police think the same killer that murdered Frank also murdered the writer?"

"The police are working on that," Angie replied carefully, not wanting to reveal too much about the ongoing investigation.

Ellie's eyes watched Kris's face. "I saw you and Lorrie Henderson at the new restaurant in Silver Cove the other evening," she said, her tone neutral but her focus intense.

Kris blinked a few times, her expression blank. For a moment, it seemed as if she might deny it, but then she nodded slowly. "Oh, right. I went there for dinner by myself. I had to get out of the house. Lorrie was there, too. She came over to my table to talk for a little while."

"What did you talk about?" Angie asked, trying to keep her voice casual.

Kris's eyes darted away, focusing on a point just over Angie's shoulder. "I really wanted to be alone and I told her so, but she stayed to ask me some questions: why we moved here; did we know that woman who was killed forty years ago; did Frank have any idea who killed her."

She waved her hand dismissively, but there was tension in her movements that hadn't been there before. "I wasn't in the mood to be questioned. I wanted to sit quietly and eat my dinner. I have no patience for anything since Frank was killed. She annoyed me. I had the waiter box my food, and I left." She sighed again, the sound heavy with fatigue and frustration. "So the answer to your question is no, I hadn't become friendly with the writer."

"Did Lorrie share any details about her research into the cold case?" Ellie pressed, sensing they might be close to something important.

"No," Kris replied sharply, her tone defensive, "and if she had, I wouldn't have remembered anything she told me. I really don't care about a forty-year-old murder. I'm living with the aftermath of my own husband's murder."

The sisters looked at each other, both noting the sudden anger in Kris's voice. There was more there than simple grief and irritation, but what?

Angie sensed they were reaching the limit of Kris's patience, but she had one more question she needed to ask. "Do you have any more insight into the messages that were included with the paper roses left near your husband?"

Kris closed her eyes for a few moments, her face a mask of exhaustion. When she opened them again, there was a hardness that hadn't been there before. "I don't have the mental energy to think about it," she said, her tone clipped and tinged with finality. "I'd like to go rest now, if you don't mind."

Recognizing the dismissal, Angie stood. "We've overstayed. We apologize. Thank you for seeing us. If you remember anything else, anything at all, please don't hesitate to call."

Ellie echoed her sister's thanks, and they made their way out of the house, the whole situation weighing on them both. As they stepped outside, the fresh air felt like a relief after the oppressive atmosphere of Kris's home.

As they climbed into their car, Angie let out a long breath. "Kris is a mess... understandably."

Ellie was quiet for a moment, her mind deep in thought. Finally, she turned to look at her sister, her expression troubled. "I don't think she's being fully upfront with us about everything. I think she might have an inkling about who killed her husband."

Angie's eyes widened in surprise. "You think she's holding back?"

"Yes, I do," Ellie replied, her voice low and serious. "Could she be protecting someone?"

The question hung in the air between them.

Angie's mind raced. "If she is," she said slowly, "who could it be?"

Ellie didn't have an answer to the question.

As they drove away from Kris's house, Angie knew that somewhere in Sweet Cove, a killer was walking free, their identity hidden behind a veil of secrets and half-truths.

20

The late afternoon was warm and sunny as the Roseland family pulled into the bustling parking area of Lilac Hill Farm. The air was filled with the sweet scent of apples and the distant notes of a fiddle, promising an evening of festivity and fun. Colorful banners fluttered in the gentle breeze, and the excited chatter of festival-goers created a buzz of anticipation.

Angie climbed out of the van, stretching her arms above her head and taking in a deep breath of the early autumn air.

"I can't believe we're finally here," she said, a smile spreading across her face. "We've been so busy lately, I almost forgot what it was like to just relax."

Josh wrapped an arm around her waist, planting

a kiss on her cheek. "Well, this afternoon and tonight are all about fun. No work, no worries, just family time."

Their daughter, Gigi, was already bouncing with excitement, her pigtails bobbing as she tugged on Angie's hand. "Mommy, can we go on the hay ride? Please, please, please?"

Courtney laughed, linking arms with Rufus. "I think we have a full evening ahead of us," she said, her eyes twinkling with amusement. "We might need to draw up a schedule to fit everything in."

The rest of the family gathered around - Ellie and Jack, Jenna and Tom with their daughter Libby, and bringing up the rear, Mr. Finch leaning on his cane and escorting his girlfriend, Betty Hayes. The group made quite a sight, a joyful parade of familiar faces heading toward the festival grounds.

As they approached the entrance, they were greeted by even more colorful decorations and the cheerful sounds of laughter and music. The Moon Festival was in full swing with families and couples milling about, enjoying the various attractions.

"Oh, look," Ellie exclaimed, pointing to a nearby field. "They've set up game booths. Who's up for a little friendly competition?"

Tom grinned, a competitive glint in his eye.

"You're on. Last one there buys the first round of cider."

With that, the group split up, some heading for the games while others were drawn to the enticing smells coming from the food trucks lined up near the barn.

Angie hurried over to the ring toss booth, Gigi perched on her hip as she aimed for the bottles. "Come on, sweetheart," she encouraged, "help Mommy win that big teddy bear!"

Nearby, Mr. Finch was trying his hand at the strength test, much to Betty's amusement. "Go on, Victor," she cheered, "show these youngsters how it's done."

To everyone's surprise and delight, Mr. Finch managed to ring the bell, earning himself a stuffed unicorn, which he promptly presented to a beaming Betty.

"Mr. Finch, you've been holding out on us," Jack teased, flexing his own muscles. "I didn't know you had it in you."

Mr. Finch chuckled, a mischievous twinkle in his eye. "There's more to me than meets the eye, my boy. A gentleman never reveals all his secrets."

Meanwhile, Jenna and Tom had discovered a face-painting booth. Libby was getting a beautiful butterfly design on her cheek, while Tom had surprisingly agreed to have a fierce tiger painted on his face.

"Dad, you look silly." Libby giggled, pointing at her father's transformation.

Tom growled playfully, chasing his daughter around in circles as she squealed with delight. Jenna watched them, her heart full of love for her little family.

As the evening progressed, they regrouped near the food trucks, arms laden with prizes and stomachs growling. The array of choices was dizzying - everything from gourmet grilled cheese sandwiches to artisanal wood-fired pizzas, and even a truck specializing in exotic fusion tacos.

"I don't know about you," Rufus said, "but I'm famished."

Soon the family had claimed a large picnic table spreading out a feast of various dishes. Ellie had opted for a vibrant Buddha bowl, while Jack couldn't resist the pulled pork sandwich. Courtney and Rufus were sharing a platter of loaded nachos, and Angie was carefully cutting up a slice of Margherita pizza for Gigi.

As they ate, the conversation flowed easily, highlighted by laughter and exclamations of delight at particularly tasty bites. For once, there was no talk of work or worries, just the simple fun of being together.

"You know," Courtney said between bites, "we should make this a yearly tradition. It's nice to have something to look forward to every autumn."

"Hear, hear!" Josh raised his cup of cider in agreement. "To new traditions and family time."

Everyone clinked their cups together, the sound mingling with the background music and chatter of the festival.

After dinner, the group made their way to the farm stand for dessert. The homemade ice cream was legendary, and the line stretched back quite a ways, but the wait was always worth it. They savored scoops of flavors like Maple Walnut, Apple Pie, and Pumpkin Spice.

"I think I've died and gone to heaven." Jenna sighed, licking her spoon clean.

"If this is heaven, I don't ever want to leave," Ellie agreed, eyeing her rapidly melting scoop of Salted Caramel Pretzel.

With sticky hands and full bellies, they decided it was time for the corn maze. The entrance loomed before them, cornstalks stretching high into the darkening sky. Strings of fairy lights had been woven through the stalks, creating a magical, twinkling path.

"All right, team," Jack said, adopting a mock-serious tone, "we go in together, we come out together. No person left behind."

Giggling, the family plunged into the maze. The rustling of the corn and the occasional startled yelp when someone took a wrong turn filled the air. Gigi and Libby led the charge, their youthful energy propelling the group forward, and sometimes backward, through the twisting paths.

"I think we've been past this scarecrow three times now," Betty observed, peering at a particularly jolly-looking straw man.

"Nonsense, my dear," Mr. Finch replied, though he didn't sound entirely convinced. "I'm sure we're making excellent progress."

After what seemed like hours but was probably only about forty-five minutes, they emerged victorious on the other side, slightly disheveled but grinning from ear to ear.

"I think we set a new record," Tom declared, checking his watch.

"Yes, for the most times getting completely turned around," Jenna teased, playfully elbowing her husband.

As twilight deepened into night, the family made their way to the apple orchard. Lanterns had been strung up between the trees, creating a magical glow over the rows of branches. The air was filled with the sweet scent of ripe apples and the soft chirping of crickets.

"Remember, everyone," Angie called out, "only pick what you can carry."

Soon, soft thuds when apples were being placed into baskets could be heard, along with an occasional crunch as someone couldn't resist taking a bite of their freshly picked fruit.

Mr. Finch helped Betty onto a wooden stool to reach a particularly tempting apple higher up in one of the trees, and as she plucked it free, she lost her balance slightly, falling back into his arms with a laugh as the two of them almost tumbled to the ground.

"My hero," she said, planting a kiss on his cheek, causing Mr. Finch to blush like a schoolboy.

"Mr. Finch, you old romantic," Josh teased good-naturedly. "You're putting the rest of us to shame."

As the evening drew to a close, the family made their way to a small hill overlooking the lake. They spread out blankets on the grass, settling in for the promised fireworks display. The moon, nearly full, shined a shimmering, silvery light over the landscape and the surface of the lake.

"Look, Mommy!" Gigi pointed excitedly at the sky. "The first star."

"Make a wish, sweetheart," Angie said softly, hugging her daughter close.

The first rockets screamed into the sky just as the full moon was rising over the lake. The explosion of colors against the night sky drew gasps and applause from the crowd.

Angie leaned back against Josh's chest, Gigi curled up in her lap, already half-asleep despite the noise. She looked around at her family - Courtney and Rufus with their heads close together, whispering and laughing; Ellie and Jack hand in hand; Jenna and Tom with Libby between them; and Mr. Finch and Betty, looking as smitten as any of the younger couples.

In that moment, surrounded by the people she loved most in the world, with the October moon shining down and fireworks lighting up the sky, Angie felt a wave of contentment wash over her. Tonight, there were no mysteries to solve and no dangers to face. There was just family, love, and the simple joy of being together.

As the final fireworks faded and the crowd began

to disperse, no one was in a hurry to leave. They lingered on their blankets, pointing out constellations and sharing stories, savoring the last moments of their perfect evening.

"Look," Ellie said softly, pointing to a streak of light across the sky, "a shooting star. Quick, everyone make a wish."

They all closed their eyes for a moment, each silently making their wish. When they opened them again, they shared a look of understanding. Whatever they had wished for individually, they all knew that moments like this were the real magic in life.

Finally, as Gigi and Libby's yawns became more frequent, they packed up their things and began the slow walk back to their cars. The festival grounds were quieter now, with just the soft strains of a lone guitarist playing near the barn.

"We should do this more often," Courtney said as they reached the parking lot. "It was really fun."

There were murmurs of agreement from everyone. As they climbed into their vehicles, there was a shared feeling of renewal, of batteries recharged.

Driving home with Gigi fast asleep in the backseat and Josh humming softly along with the radio, Angie felt a sense of peace she hadn't experienced in weeks. Tomorrow, real life would resume with all its challenges and complexities, but for tonight, all was right in the world.

As they pulled into their driveway, the Victorian mansion loomed large and welcoming before them. The porch light flickered on as they approached, as if the house was welcoming them home. Angie scooped up the sleeping Gigi, breathing in the sweet scent of her daughter's hair mingled with the lingering aroma of apples and cotton candy.

"What a perfect night," Josh said softly, unlocking the front door.

A contented smile spread over her face.

As they stepped inside, carrying the memories of their magical evening with them, Angie knew that this night under the October moon would be one they'd cherish for years to come.

21

The four Roseland sisters and Mr. Finch gathered at the round table in the family room. The rich wood gleamed softly in the lamplight, the table's surface scattered with notes, photographs, and sketches related to their ongoing investigation. Euclid and Circe lounged contentedly on the nearby sofa, their sleek fur catching the light as their tails swished occasionally, as if they too were pondering the latest mystery.

Outside, the wind whistled through the trees, their leaves rustling in a soft, continuous whisper.

Courtney, her eyes narrowed in concentration, was the first to break the silence that had settled over the group. She ran a hand through her hair, pushing it back from her face as she spoke. "Let's go over the clues again," she said, her voice tinged with a hint of frustration. "I feel kind of unmoored, like I'm drifting in a sea of clues and nothing is coming together."

Jenna absently twirled a strand of her long brown hair around her finger. The soft lamplight caught the highlights in her hair, creating a halo effect around her troubled face. "I feel the same way." She sighed. "There's a lot going on, but how does it all come together? I haven't seen Karen's ghost for a while now either. I wonder why not."

Ellie, ever the practical one, leaned forward, her eyes showing determination. "Let's start at the beginning," she suggested. "Let's talk about the clues we first found."

Angie reached for a nearby notepad, flipping it open to a fresh page. "Okay," she began, pen poised over the paper, "the book *The Catcher in the Rye* was on the kitchen counter on the day Frank died. Frank did his dissertation on that book and another one, discussing similarities between them and what it all meant."

Mr. Finch cleared his throat. He leaned back in his chair, the leather creaking softly as he shifted his weight. "What about the paper flowers?" he asked.

"The killer deliberately left them around Frank Sleet's body. What clue do they provide?"

Courtney's face lit up, and she reached for one of the photos on the table, holding it under the light. "One of the flowers held the piece of paper with an excerpt of the Robert Frost poem," she said, her finger tracing the outline of the delicate paper bloom in the image. "It tells about a road diverging and that taking the road that wasn't well-traveled had made all the difference. It could mean a choice Frank made, or maybe a choice the killer made."

"And don't forget the piece of paper under the napkin holder in the Sleets' kitchen," Angie added, scribbling in her notepad. "The note made reference to Karen LeBlanc. At least we think it did. It said: 'Where Karen fell, truth will rise.'"

Jenna reached for her mug of tea, the porcelain warm against her palm. "It seemed to point to the fact that Frank and Karen's murders were linked somehow," she mused, taking a small sip of her tea.

Angie shifted in her chair, her fingers drumming lightly on the table. The rhythmic tapping seemed to punctuate her words as she spoke. "Kris Sleet told us there wasn't anything between Frank and Karen; they'd just met in a coffee shop and kept running into each other there," she reminded them. "But Frank's brother told us that Frank seemed smitten with Karen, although he didn't make a move on her because she was in a relationship with someone else."

She paused for a moment, then continued. "Karen's old boyfriend Winthrop Kelly told us his relationship with her was flagging because they both wanted different things from life. If Karen believed her relationship with Winthrop was coming to an end, maybe she dated other people while she was in Sweet Cove. Maybe she dated Frank?"

Mr. Finch reached for his own mug, the steam rising in lazy spirals as he lifted it to his lips. "Karen's friend Carolyn mentioned that a man in Sweet Cove wanted to date Karen, but Karen refused because she didn't want to complicate things," he reminded them, his voice slightly muffled by the mug.

Ellie sighed, rubbing at the back of her neck. She stood up, stretching her arms above her head as she spoke. "I wish Karen's little red notebook had been found," she said wistfully, pacing slowly around the table. "It might have contained information about how Karen was really feeling about the men around her."

Jenna's face showed an expression of frustration. The chair creaked softly under her as she adjusted her position. "I'm not sure where to go next with this investigation. Everything seems like dead ends."

Mr. Finch's face brightened slightly. He sat up straighter, his eyes full of energy. "Chief Martin told me there may be another person he wants some of us to interview," he said. "Perhaps that will provide another avenue for us to go down."

"I sure hope so," Angie said, her voice tinged with weariness. She closed her notepad with a soft thump. "I feel like we're running in circles."

As if on cue, Euclid let out a soft meow, stretching languidly on the sofa. The sound seemed to break the tension that had been building in the room. Circe, not to be outdone, stood up and arched her back in a graceful stretch before padding over to Mr. Finch, rubbing against his legs with a contented purr.

"You know what?" Courtney said suddenly, a smile playing at the corners of her mouth. She stood up, pushing her chair back with a scrape against the hardwood floor. "I think we need a break, and I know just the thing."

The others looked at her quizzically.

"Angie," she said, turning to her sister, "didn't you make a yogurt cheesecake earlier?"

Angie's face lit up with understanding. "I sure

did," she said, already rising from her chair, "and I think that's exactly what we need right now."

The group made their way to the kitchen, their footsteps echoing softly in the quiet house. The warm, inviting aroma of baked goods grew stronger with each step.

As they entered the kitchen, the homey atmosphere seemed to envelop them, pushing the worries of the case to the background, if only for a while.

Angie busied herself with slicing the cheesecake, the knife sliding smoothly through the creamy dessert. Ellie put the kettle on for tea, the click of the switch and the subsequent bubbling of water filling the air. Jenna and Courtney set about gathering plates and silverware.

Mr. Finch settled himself at the kitchen table, a contented smile on his face as he watched the sisters move around the kitchen.

Soon, they were all seated around the table with warm mugs of tea in hand and generous slices of cheesecake before them. The first bites were met with appreciative murmurs and closed eyes, the creamy texture and subtle sweetness of the dessert seeming to melt away some of their earlier frustration.

"Well, this sure makes me feel better," Courtney said, her concern about the case melting away like the cheesecake on her tongue. She grinned at Angie, raising her fork in a mock salute. "Just keep the sweets coming, sis, and we'll be all right."

Angie laughed, the sound bright and cheerful. "I'll do my best," she promised, taking a sip of her tea. "Though if I keep baking at this rate, we might all need new wardrobes soon."

"Worth it," Ellie declared, helping herself to another small slice. "Besides, all this brain work must burn energy, right?"

As they enjoyed their late-night snack, the conversation drifted away from the case, touching instead on lighter topics – updates on their various businesses, chatter about upcoming events in town, and playful banter. The tension that had filled the rooms earlier seemed to dissipate, replaced by the pleasure of being together.

Jenna regaled them with a story about a particularly challenging customer at her jewelry store, her animated gestures nearly knocking over her mug of tea. Mr. Finch chimed in with a tale from his younger days, his eyes twinkling with mischief as he described a prank gone hilariously wrong. Even the cats joined in the festive atmosphere, with Euclid attempting to sneak a lick of cheesecake when he thought no one was looking, much to everyone's amusement.

Yet even as they laughed and chatted, each of them knew that the mysteries of Karen LeBlanc and Frank Sleet still loomed large, waiting to be unraveled.

As the grandfather clock in the hallway chimed midnight, its deep, resonant tones echoing through the house, they began to clear away the dishes. The soft clink of plates and the rush of water in the sink created a soothing rhythm as they worked together, each lost in their own thoughts about the case.

As they said their goodnights and headed off to sleep, Angie turned out the lights in the kitchen, plunging the room into a soft darkness broken only by the moonlight streaming through the windows, and she couldn't help but smile. No matter how complex the mystery, no matter how far away the truth might be, they would find the answers they were looking for. It was one of the things they did best – unraveling mysteries, one clue at a time.

22

The sun hung low on the horizon as Angie and Ellie made their way along the weathered boardwalk. The salt-tinged breeze ruffled their hair as they approached the Salem seaside café where they were set to meet award-winning journalist Nick Wallis.

Rounding the corner, the café came into view – a charming, weathered building with whitewashed walls and blue trim that seemed to blend seamlessly with the sky and sea behind it. The outdoor deck, perched on stilts over the sand, offered a panoramic view of the ocean that stretched far into the distance.

It didn't take long for the sisters to spot Nick Wallis. In his mid-sixties, the journalist cut an impressive figure, even seated at one of the weather-beaten tables on the deck under a beach umbrella.

His salt and pepper hair caught the late afternoon light, and his brown eyes sparkled with energy. As Angie and Ellie approached, he stood to greet them, his tall, lean frame moving with the easy manner of an athlete.

"Ms. Roseland and Ms. Roseland, I presume?" Nick said, a warm smile crinkling the corners of his eyes as he extended his hand. "Nick Wallis. It's a pleasure to meet you both."

Angie shook his hand first, returning his smile. "Please, call me Angie, and this is my sister, Ellie. Thank you for agreeing to meet with us this afternoon."

Nick gestured for them to take a seat. "I have to say, when Chief Martin called, I was intrigued. It's not every day you're asked to revisit events from forty years ago. He told me he'd like me to follow up with you."

As they settled into their chairs, a waitress appeared to take their orders, and they each requested a cup of the café's specialty brew.

Once the waitress had left, Angie made eye contact with the man, her voice taking on a more serious tone. "Chief Martin tells us you spent time in the area forty years ago," she began, her eyes watching Nick's reactions.

Nick's expression became thoughtful. "That's right. At the time, I was doing graduate work toward a Master's degree in Journalism and Communication. Part of it required doing a summer internship through the university at the area newspaper." A fond smile played on his lips as he added, "I fell in love with the seacoast area and eventually bought a house here in Salem."

Ellie, who had been jotting down notes in a small notebook, looked up. "The chief told you they're looking into Karen LeBlanc's cold case and the murder of Professor Frank Sleet?" she questioned, her tone careful.

A shadow seemed to pass over Nick's face. "He did. I was shocked to hear of Frank's murder. It's like déjà vu, in a way, what with Karen's murder and all. Brings back a lot of memories from that summer."

"You knew both Frank and Karen?" Ellie pressed gently.

Nick's eyes took on a faraway look. "I met Frank and Karen at the coffee shop we all frequented. It was a fun time back then. People were friendly. A lot of the clientele were students at the university doing summer work."

Angie asked, "Were you close to Frank and Karen?"

Nick set down his coffee mug, taking a moment to gather his thoughts. "I wouldn't call us close," he said slowly. "We were all only there for about six weeks. We got to know each other, but it was too short a time to become close friends. When the summer was over, we were all going off in different directions."

"What did you think of Karen?" Angie probed while turning to a new page in her notebook.

A warm smile spread across Nick's face as he recalled the young woman. "Karen was cheerful, ambitious, smart, and witty. She was great to be around, always positive and upbeat."

"And what about Frank? What was he like?" Ellie chimed in.

Nick's expression turned more serious. "Frank was very committed to his work. He loved literature with a passion. He would often be immersed in his studies. He was a smart guy, knew a lot about different topics. I enjoyed talking with him."

Angie cleared her throat, hesitating for a moment before asking, "Do you think Frank and Karen were in a relationship that summer?"

Nick's eyes widened, clearly caught off guard by the idea. "That's an interesting question," he said.

"Frank and Karen seemed close. Neither one admitted to a relationship, but there were signs – the way they looked at each other, the way they bantered. They were playful and flirty in a way that could indicate wanting to be or being in a relationship." He paused, then added, "Of course, it might have just been superficial attraction. I knew Karen had a boyfriend, and Frank was seeing someone else."

Angie perked up at this. "Frank was seeing someone? Do you know who it was?"

"Yeah, it was the woman he eventually married, Kris something or other. I only met her briefly once or twice."

Ellie looked surprised, her pen pausing mid-sentence. "We thought Frank met Kris after his graduate work in Sweet Cove."

Nick shook his head, his forehead furrowing slightly. "No, he was definitely seeing Kris when we were all in the area that summer."

"Was Kris living with Frank back then?" Angie asked, her mind considering this new information.

"No, she was in Boston. She came up a few times to visit Frank."

"We didn't know that," Angie told him. "Did that come up when you talked with Chief Martin?"

Nick thought for a moment. "I don't think it did, no. It didn't seem relevant at the time, I guess."

"Karen was dating Winthrop Kelly back then," Ellie said, steering the conversation in another direction.

A chuckle escaped Nick. "That's right. I always loved that name. Winthrop. It sounded like a high-society billionaire. He came up a couple of times. Everyone called him Winny."

"How did Karen and Winthrop get along?" Angie asked.

Nick's expression darkened slightly. "They seemed kind of cold with each other. There was always a lot of tension and annoyance going on. They weren't fun to be around when they were together. It was pretty plain it was a relationship that wouldn't last." He paused, seeming to debate whether to continue, then added, "It seemed like Winny had quite the temper. Once through the coffee shop window, I saw him grab Karen's arm. Another time, I heard him screaming at her. I was always glad when he went back to Boston."

Ellie kept her voice low when she asked, "Do you think Winthrop knew Karen was interested in Frank?"

Nick shrugged, his expression grim. "Who

knows? Karen wasn't very subtle about flirting with Frank. Winny would've had to be blind not to see it. I'm sure it fanned the flames of his anger with her."

Angie, sensing they were nearing the end of their interview, decided to ask one last question. "Did you ever see Karen with a small red leather notebook?"

To their surprise, Nick chuckled. "Everyone saw Karen with that notebook. She was always scribbling in it. If you asked to see what she was writing, she'd slap it closed and put it in her bag." His eyes twinkled with the memory. "I teased her about it. She told me it was private. Some of it was like a diary, and the rest of it was story ideas. That's what she told me anyway. I never saw her without it."

As they thanked Nick for his time and made their way back to their van, Angie and Ellie's minds swirled with this new information. The sea breeze had picked up, carrying with it the hint of an evening storm, much like the storm of questions brewing in their minds.

Once inside the van, Ellie turned to Angie with an expression of confusion. "Frank was seeing Kris when he was in Sweet Cove forty years ago?" she asked as she started the engine.

Angie shook her head in disbelief. "How did we

miss that? I thought we were told Kris met Frank after he graduated with his PhD."

"We need to talk to the chief about this," Ellie said firmly. "It changes the timeline of the case."

Angie added, "And Winthrop Kelly had a temper? He yelled at Karen and grabbed her arm? It sounds like he was really angry with her. He must have realized she was interested in Frank."

A troubling thought occurred to Ellie. "Was Winthrop angry enough to kill Karen?"

Angie's face was grim as she speculated, "I wonder if his fury was ignited again when he learned Frank had moved to Sweet Cove for retirement?"

As they pulled away from the coffee shop, Ellie sighed heavily. "Another couple of twists to this story."

The drive back to Sweet Cove was filled with discussion as the sisters dissected every detail of their conversation with Nick Wallis. The revelation about Frank and Kris's relationship timeline, the disturbing information about Winthrop's temper, and the ever-present mystery of Karen's red notebook twirled in their minds like the darkening clouds gathering on the horizon.

Angie reached for her phone as Ellie pulled the

van into their driveway. "I'm going to call the chief," she said, her mind filled with questions. "We need to update him on what we've learned."

Ellie turned off the engine. "And then we need to gather the others. It's time to reassess what we know."

The Victorian mansion's windows glowed warmly in the gathering darkness, and they climbed out of the van just as the first drops of rain began to fall. The wind and rain were a fitting backdrop to the storm of information they were about to unleash.

23

Chief Martin's police cruiser pulled up in front of the Roseland house, and he got out and headed up the walkway to the mansion. The porch light flickered on automatically, casting a shaft of light over the steps as Angie opened the front door to greet him.

"Evening, Chief," she said. "Come on in. Everyone's waiting in the kitchen."

Chief Martin's face was set with serious lines as he followed Angie through the familiar hallway. The scent of fresh coffee and lingering traces of dinner filled the air, a homey contrast to the tension that seemed to radiate from the chief's demeanor.

As they entered the spacious kitchen, the scene that greeted them was one of anticipation. Ellie,

Jenna, Courtney, and Mr. Finch were gathered around the large wooden kitchen table, their faces full of curiosity and concern.

Euclid and Circe were perched regally on chairs, as if they too were part of the impromptu meeting. At the sight of Chief Martin, they leaped down gracefully, padding over to greet him with soft meows and expectant looks, and the chief obliged them with petting and scratches behind the ears.

"How about something to drink?" Ellie asked, already rising from her chair. "Coffee?"

Chief Martin's shoulders relaxed slightly at the offer. "A black coffee would be great, thanks." He set his laptop on the table.

Angie chimed in, "What about something to eat? A sandwich? A slice of cake? We have leftover spaghetti and meatballs."

The chief chuckled, patting his stomach ruefully as he sank into one of the chairs. "All too tempting, I'm afraid, but I'm going to resist. I'm trying to lose some weight, you know."

As Ellie busied herself with the coffee maker, its gentle gurgling a soothing background noise, Chief Martin flipped open his laptop. The blue glow of the screen illuminated his face.

"I have some security footage to show you," he

began, his voice taking on a more official tone. "The first one is from the grocery store where Kris Moran-Sleet went to do some shopping on the morning Frank was killed."

The Roseland sisters and Mr. Finch gathered around, their faces bathed in the soft light of the screen. Even Euclid and Circe seemed interested, perching on nearby chairs as if to get a better view.

"We've been waiting on this video for a couple of weeks," the chief explained, his fingers hovering over the keyboard. "The store had a problem retrieving it. We finally got hold of it earlier today." With a click, he started the footage.

The video was grainy, the kind of low-quality surveillance typical of small-town stores, but even through the fuzzy image, they could clearly make out Kris pushing a cart along the aisles, her movements seeming like she was in a hurry.

When the video ended, Ellie was the first to speak. "So it proves she was at the store," she said, her tone questioning.

Chief Martin's expression remained grave. "It does, but take a look at the date-time stamp." He pointed to a corner of the screen where small, digital numbers flickered.

"Oh, gosh," Courtney breathed, her eyes

widening in surprise. "She claimed to be at the store way earlier than she actually was."

Jenna, often the voice of reason, frowned slightly. "Why would she claim that though?" she mused aloud. "Maybe she got confused due to the shock of finding Frank?"

"That could be," the chief conceded, nodding slowly. "It's something I have to clarify with her." He closed the video window and opened another file. "There's something else. Look at this video. I noticed something in it when I was looking at the footage for a different case."

As the new video began to play, the family members squinted at the screen. The footage showed a sidewalk near a busy street, people moving in and out of frame as they went about their business.

Suddenly, Courtney gasped. "Wait a sec," she said, her voice filled with surprise. "Is that Winthrop Kelly?"

Chief Martin froze the frame, zooming in on a figure exiting a restaurant. "It sure is," he confirmed. "He's leaving the Greek restaurant on Main Street right here in town. When I interviewed him about Karen LeBlanc's cold case, he told me he hadn't visited Sweet Cove for a couple of years."

A heavy silence fell over the kitchen as this piece of information sank in.

Mr. Finch was the first to speak, his voice thoughtful. "Why would the man lie? When was he caught on this footage?"

The chief's answer sent a chill through the room. "The night before Frank was murdered."

Angie felt her heart racing and her breath catching in her throat. "That begs some questions," she said slowly, voicing the thoughts that were undoubtedly running through everyone's minds. "Was he still here the next morning? Did he stay overnight? And more importantly, did Winthrop Kelly kill Frank Sleet?"

Chief Martin closed his laptop with a soft click. "I have the very same questions," he said. "My team is looking into it as we speak. It's concerning because the journalist who was in town forty years ago told you about Winthrop having a temper and the aggressive way he interacted with Karen. The things the journalist said about Winthrop might cause us to consider him a suspect in Karen's murder, as well as in Frank's and Lorrie's."

The kitchen fell silent once more, the only sound the soft purring of Euclid and Circe as they wound their way around the chief's legs, ignoring the tension in the room.

"What's the next step?" Ellie asked, setting a steaming mug of coffee in front of the chief.

Chief Martin wrapped his hands around the mug, seemingly grateful for its warmth. "I'll take the train into Boston either this evening or in the morning to talk to Winthrop Kelly. The man has some explaining to do."

This new information had shifted the landscape of their investigation dramatically. Winthrop Kelly, once a peripheral figure in the case, had suddenly become central to the mystery.

"Do you think he'll cooperate?" Jenna asked, her voice tinged with concern.

The chief shrugged, his expression grim. "Hard to say. He's already lied about being in Sweet Cove. We'll have to approach this carefully."

Angie turned to her sisters. "We need to go over everything we know about Winthrop Kelly," she said. "Every interaction, every detail, no matter how small."

Courtney was already reaching for a notebook. "I'll start compiling a timeline," she said.

As the kitchen burst into a flurry of activity with the sisters diving into their notes and Mr. Finch offering his insights, Chief Martin watched with admiration. The Roseland family's dedication to solving this case was admirable, but he couldn't help but worry about the potential dangers they might be walking into.

"Just be careful," he said, his voice cutting through the buzz of conversation. "We don't know what we're dealing with here. If Winthrop Kelly is involved in these murders, he's not someone to be taken lightly."

The sisters paused in their discussion. They understood the risks, but they would still continue.

Outside, the quiet streets of Sweet Cove lay peaceful under the starry sky, unaware of what was brewing in the old Victorian mansion.

With a final word of caution to the Roseland family, Chief Martin stepped out into the cool night air, his mind already planning his approach for the upcoming interview with Winthrop Kelly. Behind him, the warm light of the kitchen spilled out onto the porch.

Angie decided to walk to the Sleet residence to get some exercise and think about the case. The crisp evening air nipped at her cheeks as she made her way down the quiet streets of Sweet Cove, and the streetlights cast long shadows across the sidewalk, pushing away the darkness that seemed to be closing in around the case.

Chief Martin's text message still burned in her mind:

> Going to Boston to speak with Winthrop Kelly. Can you swing by the Sleet house to talk to Kris? I called her to ask if I could come by tomorrow, but she told me she's going out of town for a few days.

The request had seemed simple enough at the time. Now, as Angie approached Kris Moran-Sleet's house, a sense of unease began to creep over her. She tried to shake it off, attributing it to the eeriness of the quiet neighborhood.

When she approached the house, the garage light was on, spilling a harsh fluorescent glow onto the driveway. Angie could see Kris inside working in the garage stacking boxes.

Taking a deep breath, she stepped into view.

"Hey, there," Angie called out, trying to keep her voice light and casual.

Kris jumped, clearly startled by the sudden intrusion.

Angie quickly apologized, feeling a twinge of guilt for frightening the woman. "Did the chief tell you I was going to stop by?"

"He didn't," Kris replied, wiping her hands on her jeans. There was something in her tone, a tightness that Angie couldn't quite place.

"Sorry, I thought he was going to let you know," Angie said, feeling that jolt of unease return. She glanced at the boxes surrounding Kris. "You're packing already?"

Kris's posture suddenly seemed more guarded. "Yeah. I really can't wait to get out of this house. I might be going to stay with my sister sooner than I thought."

Angie offered her assistance.

"Actually, if you don't mind, I could use some help stacking these boxes by the door," Kris told her. "A friend is coming with a truck tomorrow morning to take the stuff to storage."

"I'd be glad to give you a hand."

As they worked together, moving boxes and stacking them by the door, Angie carefully steered the conversation toward Frank.

"When did you say you met Frank?" she asked, trying to keep her tone casual.

Kris hefted another box onto the stack. "After his graduate studies were completed. I met him in DC through a mutual friend."

Angie paused, recalling the conversation with Nick Wallis. "Someone told us you were dating Frank when he was in Sweet Cove doing research at the university for his dissertation."

Something flickered across Kris's face before her expression hardened. "I was casually dating him then, but we broke it off. I didn't see him again until we both moved to DC."

Angie filed away this information. She decided to press further. "Chief Martin also wanted to check on the time you were at the market. The timestamp doesn't match when you said you were there."

Kris's movements faltered for a moment. "I don't know. Maybe I was mixed up about the time. I don't even remember now."

"The chief just wanted to clear up the confusion," Angie assured her, while inwardly, her suspicions were growing.

Kris mumbled something about needing more packing tape and disappeared into the house. Angie continued moving boxes, her mind thinking over the situation and why she felt so anxious.

As she turned to lift another box, she heard a crash. One of the top boxes had slipped off the stack, some of its contents spilling onto the garage floor.

"Oh, darn," Angie muttered, bending down to gather the fallen items. Suddenly, she froze. There, among the scattered belongings, was a small, red leather notebook.

Time seemed to stand still as Angie stared at the notebook, her heart pounding hard.

There it was - Karen LeBlanc's missing notebook.

A noise from behind her made Angie look up. Kris stood in the doorway, her eyes fixed on the scene before her. The look on her face sent a chill down Angie's spine.

"Did the box rip open?" Kris asked, her voice unnaturally calm.

Angie tried to keep her voice steady. "Yeah. It's okay though. Nothing broke." She reached down, attempting to gather the items quickly.

"Don't bother," Kris said, her voice as cold as ice.

Angie looked up to see Kris pointing a gun directly at her. The world seemed to tilt as the reality of what was happening hit her. Her stomach lurched, and for a moment, she thought she might be sick.

"Move to the back of the garage. Now!" Kris shouted, her earlier composure cracking.

On shaky legs, Angie complied, her mind racing for a way out. She watched as Kris, her eyes never leaving Angie, reached for the garage door control. As the door began to lower, Angie's heart sank. She knew what was coming next.

Suddenly, the door's descent halted. Both women looked toward the entrance, confusion etched on their faces. There, sitting calmly in the garage doorway, was Euclid.

The large orange cat let out a bone-chilling hiss, his fur standing on end.

Before either woman could react, Mr. Finch appeared behind Euclid, leaning on his cane. Circe slunk in beside him, her green eyes glowing in the harsh garage light.

Mr. Finch was wearing a jacket, and his hand was in his pocket. It looked like he had a gun in his pocket and was pointing it right at Kris.

"I'm an older man," Mr. Finch said, his voice steady and calm, "but I was a sharpshooter in the Marines, and I go to the firing range every week to keep up my skills. If I were you, I'd drop your weapon. I wouldn't bet against me."

As Mr. Finch spoke, Angie's survival instincts kicked in. She inched toward a rack of garden tools hanging on the wall, her hand slowly reaching for a long-handled shovel.

Kris laughed, a harsh, brittle sound. "I doubt you have a weapon in that pocket of yours, old man."

Mr. Finch calmly withdrew his hand, revealing a gun. "Drop your weapon," he ordered. "You cannot beat me."

For a moment, the garage was filled with a tense silence. Then, everything happened at once.

Kris raised her gun, aiming at Mr. Finch. In a blur of fur and claws, Euclid and Circe launched themselves at the woman. Simultaneously, Angie swung the shovel with all her might, connecting solidly with Kris's legs.

A shot rang out, the bullet embedding itself harmlessly in the ceiling. In the chaos that followed, Angie managed to kick the gun away from Kris and use her own belt to bind the woman's hands behind her back.

While Mr. Finch was dialing the police emergency number, Angie

reached out to hug the cats and then stood on

weak legs. As the adrenaline began to ebb, Mr. Finch wrapped her in a hug.

"Are you all right, Miss Angie?" he asked, his voice filled with concern.

Tears of relief streamed down her face. "I'm fine. I wasn't expecting the cavalry to come save me." She looked up at Mr. Finch, a question forming on her lips. "Where on earth did you get a gun?"

Mr. Finch's eyes twinkled with mischief. "It's fake. It's just plastic. It was one of the props Courtney and Rufus used when they dressed as gangsters for the Halloween party last year."

Angie felt the color drain from her face. "Mr. Finch, you came in here unarmed. You could have been killed."

Mr. Finch simply smiled. "But I wasn't. And neither were you. That was our mission, and it was completed successfully." His face grew serious as he looked deep into Angie's eyes. "I would give my life to save yours, Miss Angie. I would do that for any of you."

As the sound of approaching sirens filled the air, fresh tears sprang to Angie's eyes. She held tight to Mr. Finch, never wanting to let him go.

24

Later that night, the lights in the Victorian's windows cut through the darkness, a beacon of safety and comfort after the harrowing events at the Sleet residence. As Angie, Mr. Finch, and the cats stepped onto the familiar porch, the door flew open, revealing the anxious faces of the Roseland family.

"Angie!" Josh cried, pulling his wife into a tight embrace.

Courtney hurried over and held her sister. "We've been so worried."

The family room was a flurry of activity as they all settled in, everyone eager to hear about what had happened. Angie sank into her favorite armchair, feeling exhausted by the evening's events. Mr. Finch took his usual seat, his normally neat appearance slightly disheveled, but his eyes twinkled with joy at their narrow escape.

"All right," Ellie said, her voice carrying the no-nonsense tone she often used in difficult situations. "We need to hear everything. From the beginning."

Angie took a deep breath, her gaze sweeping across the concerned faces of her loved ones. "Kris Moran-Sleet was arrested tonight," she began, her voice steady despite the lingering shock. "For murdering her husband Frank and Lorrie ... and for killing Karen LeBlanc."

A collective gasp went up from the group.

Jenna eyes went wide. "She killed both of them? But how? Why?"

As Angie explained the events at the garage, from the discovery of the red notebook to Kris pulling a gun on her, the room fell into a tense silence, broken only by the occasional gasp or murmur of disbelief.

When she finished, all eyes turned to Mr. Finch.

"How on earth did you know to go to Angie's rescue?" Tom asked, his arm wrapped protectively around Jenna.

Mr. Finch straightened in his chair, a proud smile playing at the corners of his mouth. "I was painting in my sunroom when Circe and Euclid came in howling and screeching," he explained. "They pawed crazily at the windows, tried to climb the drapes, and kept rushing to me in distress. I knew right away that Angie must be in trouble."

He paused, reaching down to scratch behind Euclid's ears as the cat rubbed against his legs. "I moved as fast as I could into the kitchen, grabbed the keys to Ellie's van, and then the cats and I raced outside to the vehicle. Before I did that though, I'd had the idea to take the plastic gun with me."

"Why didn't you ask Josh for help?" Angie asked.

"Josh and Gigi had gone to Tom and Jenna's house for ice cream sundaes," Mr. Finch explained. "I couldn't wait. There was no time to lose."

Angie shook her head in wonder, tears pricking at the corners of her eyes. "Thank the heavens you showed up when you did. If you hadn't..." Her voice trailed off, unable to complete the thought.

Mr. Finch reached out, patting her hand gently. "We won't even think about alternate outcomes," he said firmly. "You're safe, Miss Angie, and that's all that matters."

"My hero," Angie said softly, bringing Mr. Finch's hand to her lips and kissing it gently.

Euclid let out a loud meow, as if indignant at

being left out of the praise. Circe, not to be outdone, trilled loudly from her perch on the back of the sofa.

Angie laughed, the sound breaking the last of the tension in the room. "You're my heroes, too," she told the cats, getting up to envelop them both in a hug. "Thank you for saving me."

As the initial shock of the evening's events began to wear off, the family's natural curiosity took over. Questions flew back and forth across the room, each person trying to piece together the complex puzzle that had finally been solved.

"But why did Kris kill Karen all those years ago?" Courtney asked. "And why Frank now?"

Angie sighed, settling back into her chair. "I guess Kris was jealous of Karen's relationship with Frank back then. She probably thought Karen was trying to steal Frank away from her. We'll know more when Chief Martin sorts through everything."

A heavy silence fell over the room as they all contemplated the tragic consequences of Kris's jealousy.

"And Frank?" Jenna asked softly. "Why kill him after all these years?"

Mr. Finch shook his head sadly. "We'll have to wait for Chief Martin's report, but he told us Frank had discovered Karen's notebook and confronted his wife with it."

As the family continued to discuss the case, piecing together details of the mystery, there was a sense of closure settling over the room.

Outside, the first hints of dawn were beginning to color the sky. Angie stood, moving to the window to watch as the new day began. She felt someone beside her and turned to see Mr. Finch, his kind eyes filled with understanding.

"It's over, Miss Angie," he said softly. "Karen and Frank can rest in peace now."

Angie felt a weight lift from her shoulders. "Thank you, Mr. Finch. For everything."

As the sun rose over Sweet Cove, bathing the town in warm morning light, the Roseland family gathered closer. The mystery was solved, justice would be served, and their life in their beloved town could return to normal.

But as Angie looked around at her family and at Euclid and Circe curled up contentedly on the sofa, she knew that "normal" for the Roselands would always include a bit of mystery, a dash of adventure, and a whole lot of love.

The warm autumn sun filtered through the stained-glass windows of the Victorian's study as Chief Martin sat in one of the high-backed leather chairs, his face softened by the play of light and shadow. The Roseland sisters, along with Mr. Finch, gathered around, waiting to hear the full story behind the murders.

Chief Martin cleared his throat, his voice taking on the measured tone of a man who had seen too much in his years of service. "We've finally been able to piece together what happened," he began, his eyes sweeping across the attentive faces before him. "It all goes back to forty years ago when Kris visited Frank in Sweet Cove."

The room fell silent as the chief told them the tragic tale of jealousy, obsession, and murder. He spoke of how Kris had seen the attraction between Frank and Karen, how Frank had tried to deny it, and how Kris had been devastated by what she perceived as a betrayal.

"Frank told Kris he wasn't seeing Karen, which was true because Karen wasn't interested enough to date him," Chief Martin explained, "but Frank was practically obsessed with Karen, and Kris could see that as plain as day."

Angie shook her head, her voice barely above a whisper. "So that's why she did it? Out of jealousy?"

The chief said, "Kris broke into Karen's place and murdered her. She stole the young woman's red leather notebook, where she read Karen's entries about Frank pursuing her."

"But Frank didn't know what Kris had done?" Jenna asked, her eyes wide with disbelief.

"No, he didn't," Chief Martin confirmed. "He and Kris eventually broke up. Kris moved to DC, and a couple of years later, Frank moved there as well. They met again at a party thrown by a mutual friend, and about a year later, they married."

The sisters looked at each other, each imagining the weight of such a terrible secret carried for so many years.

"When Frank suggested retiring to Sweet Cove," the chief continued, "he had to work hard to convince Kris to move there, but finally she agreed."

"That must have been torture for her," Ellie mused, "living in the place where she'd committed such a horrible crime."

Chief Martin said, "It all came to a head when they moved into their new home. Kris and Frank had a terrible fight over Karen and Frank's lingering feelings for her. Frank had found the red notebook in his wife's things. In her fury, Kris admitted to Frank that she was the one who'd killed Karen."

Everyone shook their heads.

Mr. Finch's eyes widened. "And that's when she killed Frank?"

"Exactly," the chief confirmed. "Horrified that it had slipped out, Kris got her gun and shot him to death before he could call the police."

"But what about the paper flowers?" Courtney asked. "And the book in the kitchen?"

"Ah, that was all part of her cover-up," Chief Martin explained. "She'd taken a class on making paper flowers while in DC and had some in the house. She placed them around the body, wrote the notes about Karen and the road not taken, and placed one of her husband's favorite books in the kitchen – all to make it seem like some kind of literary murder."

"What about Lorrie?" Courtney asked.

The chief said, "Lorrie was getting too close to putting the pieces together. Kris knew she'd figure out sooner than later that Kris was the killer so she had to silence the writer."

As the chief finished his explanation, silence fell over the room. The tragedy that had unfolded over four decades seemed to press down on all of them.

"What a mess," Angie finally said, shaking her head in disbelief.

Ellie's voice was soft, tinged with both pity and horror. "Kris is seriously disturbed. I hope she gets the help she needs."

As Chief Martin prepared to leave, thanking the Roseland family for their help in solving the case, Courtney asked, "What about Winthrop Kelly? Why did he lie to you about the last time he'd been in Sweet Cove?"

"When I went to see him, he'd admitted he'd had dinner with friends in town here. He thought my question meant had he stayed in town for a vacation. He was very apologetic for the misunderstanding."

As October drew to a close, the Roseland family decided it was time for a celebration. The backyard of the mansion was transformed into a festive wonderland for a grand cookout, with colorful streamers and twinkling lights strung between the old oak trees. The day dawned bright and clear, a perfect autumn day with a beautiful blue sky stretching endlessly overhead.

Chairs and tables were scattered across the lawn,

dressed in cheerful checkered tablecloths. Lawn games – cornhole, horseshoes, and a giant Jenga set – were set up for the guests' enjoyment. The air was filled with the tantalizing aroma of grilling meat and veggies and the sound of laughter and cheerful conversation.

Angie stood by the refreshment table surveying the scene with a contented smile. Her family and friends mingled happily, their faces bright with joy and relaxation. It was a far cry from the tension and worry that had gripped them all.

"Quite a turnout," Josh said, coming up beside her and wrapping an arm around her waist.

Angie leaned into him, grateful for his caring, steady presence. "It's perfect," she replied. "Just what we all needed."

Across the lawn, Courtney and Rufus were engaged in an intense game of cornhole, their competitive spirits on full display. Jenna and Tom cheered them on from the sidelines, with little Libby perched on her father's shoulders.

Ellie and Jack had taken charge of the grill, working in perfect tandem to keep the burgers, hot dogs, and vegetable skewers coming. The scent of sizzling meat and charred vegetables floated through the air, making everyone's mouths water in anticipation.

With Euclid and Circe squeezed into the chair with him, Mr. Finch held court near the dessert table, regaling a group of enthralled listeners with tales of his younger days. His eyes twinkled with mischief as he described some particularly daring escapades, causing his audience to burst into laughter.

As the afternoon wore on, guests moved from game to game, their laughter and chatter creating a happy noise. Children ran about, their shrieks of delight adding to the festive atmosphere. Even Euclid and Circe got into the spirit, prancing about the yard and accepting pats and treats from admiring guests.

When dinner was finally served, everyone gathered around the long tables, plates piled high with grilled delights and an array of colorful salads. The clinking of glasses and the hum of conversation filled the air as friends and neighbors caught up with each other, sharing stories and laughter.

As the sun began to set, Angie found herself overwhelmed with gratitude. She looked around at her family – her sisters, their husbands, the children,

Mr. Finch, the two cats – and felt a surge of love so strong it nearly brought tears to her eyes.

They had been through so much together, faced dangers, solved mysteries that had seemed impossible, and yet here they were, stronger than ever.

As darkness fell, the party began to wind down. Guests departed with full bellies and happy hearts, leaving behind a chorus of thank yous and promises to get together again soon.

Finally, it was just the family left, and they gathered around the fire pit together. Rufus delighted everyone by using his fire power to light the logs, and when the flames caught, the flickering light reflected over their faces. Euclid and Circe curled up nearby, their eyes shining in the firelight as they watched over their humans.

Angie looked around at her loved ones – Courtney and Rufus snuggled together on a bench, Jenna and Tom with sleepy Libby between them, Ellie and Jack hand in hand, and Mr. Finch in his favorite chair, a contented smile on his face. Josh sat beside her, their fingers intertwined, while Gigi dozed in his lap.

"I'd say this was a success," Ellie said, her voice soft in the quiet of the night.

"More than a success," Jenna agreed. "It was perfect."

As they sat there, watching the flames dance and the stars twinkle overhead, Angie felt a deep sense of peace settle over her. The mysteries were solved, justice had been served, and here they were, together and safe.

"You know," Mr. Finch said, his voice carrying the weight of wisdom, "life is full of mysteries. Some we solve, but what matters most are not the mysteries themselves, but the people we have beside us as we face them."

The others murmured in agreement, each lost in their own thoughts.

"So," Courtney said after a moment, a mischievous glint in her eye, "who's ready for our next adventure?"

Laughter erupted around the fire pit, warm and genuine, because they all knew that whatever came next – be it mystery, danger, or just the everyday challenges of life – they would face it side by side.

As the fire burned low and the night grew late, the Roseland family remained there, surrounded by the love and warmth they had created together. And in that moment, all was right in their world.

THANK YOU FOR READING! RECIPES BELOW!

Books by J.A. WHITING can be found here:
amazon.com/author/jawhiting

To hear about new books and book sales, please sign up for my mailing list at:
jawhiting.com

Your email will never be sold, shared, or spammed.

If you enjoyed the book, please consider leaving a review. A few words are all that's needed. It would be very much appreciated.

BOOKS BY J. A. WHITING

SWEET COVE PARANORMAL COZY MYSTERIES

SPELLBOUND BOOKSHOP PARANORMAL COZY MYSTERIES

LIN COFFIN PARANORMAL COZY MYSTERIES

CLAIRE ROLLINS PARANORMAL COZY MYSTERIES

MURDER POSSE PARANORMAL COZY MYSTERIES

PAXTON PARK PARANORMAL COZY MYSTERIES

ELLA DANIELS WITCH COZY MYSTERIES

SEEING COLORS PARANORMAL COZY MYSTERIES

OLIVIA MILLER MYSTERIES (not cozy)

SWEET ROMANCES by JENA WINTER

COZY BOX SETS

BOOKS BY J.A. WHITING & NELL MCCARTHY

HOPE HERRING PARANORMAL COZY MYSTERIES

TIPPERARY CARRIAGE COMPANY COZY MYSTERIES

BOOKS BY J.A. WHITING & ARIEL SLICK

GOOD HARBOR WITCHES PARANORMAL COZY MYSTERIES

BOOKS BY J.A. WHITING & AMANDA DIAMOND

PEACHTREE POINT COZY MYSTERIES

DIGGING UP SECRETS PARANORMAL COZY
MYSTERIES

BOOKS BY J.A. WHITING & MAY STENMARK

MAGICAL SLEUTH PARANORMAL WOMEN'S FICTION COZY MYSTERIES

HALF MOON PARANORMAL MYSTERIES

VISIT US

jawhiting.com

bookbub.com/authors/j-a-whiting

amazon.com/author/jawhiting

facebook.com/jawhitingauthor

bingebooks.com/author/ja-whiting

SOME RECIPES FROM THE SWEET COVE SERIES

Recipes

PUFF AND FLUFF YOGURT CAKE

INGREDIENTS

1 cup plain yogurt

1 cup granulated sugar

½ cup canola oil

2 cups all-purpose flour

3 large eggs

1½ teaspoons baking powder

½ teaspoon baking soda

1 teaspoon vanilla extract

DIRECTIONS

Preheat your oven to 350°F (175°C). Grease and flour a 9-inch round cake pan.

In a large mixing bowl, whisk together the yogurt, sugar, and vegetable oil until well combined.

Add the eggs one at a time, beating well after each addition. Stir in the vanilla extract.

In a separate bowl, whisk together the flour, baking powder, and baking soda.

Gradually add the dry ingredients to the wet ingredients, mixing until just combined. Be careful not to overmix.

Pour the batter into the prepared cake pan and smooth the top.

Bake in the preheated oven for about 30-35 minutes, or until a toothpick inserted into the center comes out clean.

Once done, remove the cake from the oven and let it cool in the pan for 10 minutes. Then, transfer the cake to a wire rack to cool completely.

Dust the cake with powdered sugar or add a dollop of whipped cream.

PEAR FRITTATA

INGREDIENTS

2 firm-ripe pears (about a pound in total)

2 Tablespoon butter

6 large eggs

⅓ cup milk

¼ cup all-purpose flour

1 Tablespoon sugar

1 teaspoon vanilla

¼ teaspoon salt

¼ cup mascarpone cheese or whipped cream cheese

1-2 Tablespoons firmly packed brown sugar

DIRECTIONS

Rinse, peel and core pears. Cut into ½ inch chunks

In a 9–10-inch, oven-proof frying pan, over medium heat, melt the butter. Add the pears. Turn occasionally until lightly browned and tender when pierced, about 7-8 minutes.

Meanwhile, in a bowl, whisk to blend: eggs, milk, flour, sugar, vanilla and salt.

Remove frying pan from heat and pour egg mixture over the pears.

Bake in a 425°F oven until the frittata is golden brown and set in the center when the pan is gently shaken. About 8-12 minutes

Cut into wedges to serve. Spoon dollops of cheese onto portions and sprinkle with brown sugar.

KEY LIME PIE

INGREDIENTS FOR CRUST

I½ cups graham cracker crumbs

4 Tablespoons sugar

6 Tablespoons melted butter

INGREDIENTS FOR PIE FILLING

3 cups sweetened condensed milk

½ cup sour cream

½ cup fresh lime juice

¼ cup fresh lemon juice

I Tablespoon grated lime zest

Lime slices

Whipped cream

DIRECTIONS

In medium-sized bowl, mix graham cracker crumbs, sugar, and melted butter until well-blended.

Press into a 9-inch pie plate.

Bake at 375°F for about 7 minutes.

Chill crust for 1 hour.

Reduce heat to 350°F.

In a medium bowl, mix condensed milk, sour cream, lime juice, and lemon juice.

Pour filling into chilled pie crust and bake for 15 minutes or until almost set. Tiny bubbles should show on the surface, but do not let the pie brown.

Let cool.

Garnish with lime slices and whipped cream.

BERRY AND CUSTARD

INGREDIENTS

Butter (for the dish)

1 cup fresh blueberries

1 cup fresh raspberries

3 eggs

½ granulated sugar

1 cup whole milk

¼ cup heavy cream

1½ teaspoons vanilla extract

½ cup flour

Pinch of salt

Confectioners or powdered sugar

DIRECTIONS

Preheat oven to 375°F.

Generously butter a 9 or 10-inch deep dish ceramic pie plate or another round or oval 2-quart dish.

Arrange berries in a single layer in the baking dish.

In a large bowl, whisk eggs (or use an electric hand-held mixer). Add sugar and whisk or beat for 1 minute until slightly frothy. Whisk in milk, cream, and vanilla. Whisk in flour and salt. Blend well until batter is smooth.

Slowly pour the batter over the berries. Transfer to oven and bake 40-45 minutes until top is set, slightly puffed, and lightly golden around the edges. A toothpick inserted in the center should come out clean when removed.

Let the dish sit for 15 minutes, or until custard is no longer hot.

Sprinkle with powdered or confectioner's sugar.

May serve warm or cooled. Spoon onto plates.

Berry and Custard

Enjoy!

Made in United States
North Haven, CT
16 October 2024

58992194R00193